An Angel's Song

by

Sharon Saracino

The Earthbound Series, Volume 4

An Angel's Song

COPYRIGHT © 2016 by Sharon Saracino

Cover Art by *Debbie Taylor*

The Wild Rose Press, Inc.
PO Box 708
Adams Basin, NY 14410-0708
Visit us at www.thewildrosepress.com

Publishing History
First Fantasy Rose Edition, 2016
Print ISBN 978-1-5092-1080-0
Digital ISBN 978-1-5092-1081-7

The Earthbound Series, Volume 4
Published in the United States of America

"Tessa..."

he stepped toward her and held out a hand.

"Don't you touch me," she warned, taking a quick step back, eyeing him warily.

Okay, so maybe he'd been an oblivious jackass. Hardly the first time, but maybe it showed progress if he'd noticed without someone else pointing it out?

"Look, I could have warned you, but frankly it just never occurred to me. You've had a long night, and you're tired and hurting. I get it. I'm not happy about this, but believe it or not, I really am trying to help. I'm not the bad guy here."

"Meaning I am?" She spat, stepping right up toe to toe, crossing her arms over her chest, and craning her neck to look directly into his face. "I fly thousands of miles, watch my father die, and then, before I can even process what that means, I am grabbed by *you*, of all people, and spirited off against my will without so much as a by-your-leave. And you have the audacity to stand there and tell me *you're* not happy about this?"

Alec decided he definitely preferred angry Tessa. Her eyes deepened to the swirling blue of an angry sea and her chest heaved, straining the buttons of the wrinkled white blouse and thrusting her high breasts against the thin fabric. With her bright eyes snapping, red-gold curls tumbling over her shoulders, and her cheeks hot and flushed, pissed or not, she was freakin' magnificent.

Dedications

Thank you to my editor, Frances Sevilla
who cheers me on, sets me straight,
and polishes the rough stones to make them shine.
~*~
Thank you to the amazing team at
The Wild Rose Press who are a joy to work with.
~*~
And to my readers,
thank you for believing in angels…
especially those of the Earthbound persuasion.
Alec and Tessa's story showcases the power of love
and the magic of second chances.
This one's for you.

Chapter One

"Speechless, Alec? It isn't like you to show such restraint," Michael the Archangel drawled.

Alec McAllister continued to stare out of the mullioned window of the *Castel Sant'Angelo*, a slight shrug the only indication he'd heard. Concentrating on the easy, regular sound of his breathing as the long minutes ticked by, he allowed no outward hint of his inner turmoil as he feigned interest in the picturesque view of the late day picnickers in the *Parco Adriano* through the wavy glass of Michael's quarters. Over the centuries, the hulking cylindrical landmark on the banks of the Tiber served as the mausoleum for an emperor and a bastion against invaders for the princes of the church before its current role as a tourist attraction and museum. Alec wondered if Hadrian would be pleased or appalled at the changes wrought by the passing years. The fact it also doubled as the headquarters for the *Defensori,* the military arm of the *Earthbound,* and did duty as the earthly abode of their commander was far less widely known.

"What exactly do you expect me to say?" Alec ground out between clenched teeth. "Do you have any idea what you're asking?"

The expensive leather creaked as Michael shifted his position on the enormous sectional sofa whose modernity contrasted sharply with the renaissance décor of his chambers. Alec turned to face him, eyes narrowed. Most were intimidated by the Archangel. His size alone was daunting, straining the seams of his custom Italian designer jacket, but Alec knew far too much about his past to be overly intimidated.

"Technically, I'm not the one asking."

Alec barked, a short laugh which held no mirth. He straightened to his full height of well over six feet, and looked down his nose at the angelic military commander. Michael simply stared back expectantly, legs crossed, looking as unruffled and relaxed as if he'd invited Alec to stop by for lunch.

"Old age must have affected his mind," Alec spat as though tasting something foul. His voice cracked only slightly. Then he stepped away from the window and paced the expansive parlor.

"I know you're feeling a bit put out right now. But, I'm simply the messenger."

A bit put out? Alec fumed silently. Such a master of understatement. Alec felt Michael's gaze following him as he continued to struggle, stalking the confines of the large room, trying to absorb and process everything he'd just learned. A thought struck him. He spun to face the Archangel.

"Maybe Dimitri can..." Alec began, but Michael shook his head.

"Dimitri Radchenko is a gifted healer, but this is beyond even his skill. I'm sorry, Alec."

"Well, whether or not I'm willing is a moot point. She made her feelings clear a long time ago." Alec growled as he stopped his pacing and resumed staring out the window. He stood still and silent, lost in thoughts of that night long ago as dusk swallowed the sun, zipping up the sky like an old gray sweater.

"So you'll do it?" Michael rose so swiftly and gracefully from the depths of the sofa it would have appeared magical to anyone else, and came to stand behind Alec.

"I want to see him," Alec announced turning to face the larger man.

"Alec, I don't think…after all these years what purpose would it serve? He isn't what he was. You won't even recognize—" Alec brought his palm up in a speak-to-the-hand gesture and Michael stammered to a halt.

"I know his soul. And I still say he can't be in his right mind to suggest this."

"Why not? She's your wife. Maybe it's time the two of you sat down and talked. And besides, you never know when her gifts could be useful to us…er, you. I'm only thinking of the greater good."

"Your own good, you mean," Alec snapped, referring to Michael's quest to retrieve the collection of supernatural objects the Archangel had secretly created millennia ago to protect his daughter from his enemies following the revocation of her immortality. "You asked for my help and my discretion all these years and you got it. To the exclusion of everything else in my life. And yeah, that's on me. But, I've seen some of your toys in action, and the damage they can inflict. Taking them out of circulation is the only option. You want me to agree to this? I want to see Barachiel and speak to him myself. That's my condition."

If Michael could be believed—and realistically why would he lie about it at this point—Barachiel wouldn't last the night. And now, as Barachiel prepared to depart this Earth, he asked Alec be there for Contessa in her grief. Even after ten years, the wound sometimes felt as fresh and raw as the day she walked away. The belated realization he drove her to it cut even deeper. Still, he couldn't deny a friend this last measure of peace. Maybe the time *had* come for him and Tessa to have a conversation. Then again, maybe there was nothing left to say. Regardless, he would stand by her through this loss. It was the right thing to do. Whether he did it for the right reasons was something Alec chose not to examine too closely at the moment.

"Fine, let's go." Michael pounded him on the shoulder and moved toward the door. Alec swallowed over the thick lump in his throat and nodded back wondering how he would say good-bye.

*****

Contessa stretched and twisted the stiffness from her neck, wincing at the audible crack. Then she dropped her head against the back of the seat. The plane descended quickly, bumping and jolting on the tarmac, before screeching to a stop on the darkened runway at *Fiumicino*. Her father. Dying. She could not fathom it. She always thought it would take nothing short of Armageddon to bring her big, strapping father down. And she never believed it could happen so quickly.

Hitching her backpack over the shoulder of her white cotton blouse, she quickly exited the plane, ignored the cheerful *buonasera* from the flight attendant, and hurried through customs. She headed straight for the double wide row of cabs idling in an expectant line outside the terminal doors. She had the address of the apartment on *Borgo Pio* in her pocket, but she would go directly to the hospital. No matter what her father said, she'd learned to trust in her dreams. At first the dreams were beautiful, consisting of lights, colors, and whispers dancing just beyond her reach, twirling, twinkling, and teasing with secrets she couldn't quite grasp. Over the years, they'd not only increased in frequency, they'd evolved into something dark and anxious, thick and suffocating, threatening, deep, and empty. Filled with incoherent whispers and disjointed suggestions of danger, they'd crashed down upon her last night, one on top of the other. It must mean there wasn't much time.

The hard knot building just below the notch in her collarbone during the nearly nine hour flight over the Atlantic, grew exponentially larger as the minutes ticked by, making it painfully difficult to breathe. Everything around her seemed irrelevant tonight. The world would be here tomorrow, and next week, and long into the foreseeable future. The world would go on. Her father would not. She'd grown accustomed to keeping people at a distance and didn't realize until now exactly how isolated she allowed herself to become. Just for tonight she wished she had someone, anyone to hold her close and tell her she was not about to lose the only person in the world to whom she meant anything. Someone to tell her she wouldn't be left truly alone.

The characteristic humidity of the Roman summer smacked her in the face and sucked the breath from her lungs as she stepped from the air conditioned terminal into the thick twilight swirling with the exhaust fumes of idling vehicles. A thin film of moisture slicked her skin as she sprinted to the first cab in the line and reached for the door. She ignored the look the driver gave her gloved hands. He certainly wasn't the first person in the world to regard her curiously. In fact, he wasn't even the first person today. Glancing down, she both blessed and cursed the talent contained in the fingers encased in heavy flesh-colored cotton. She reached out again and yanked at the door handle, tossing her backpack on the seat, and then she climbed in behind it.

Exquisitely sensitive, nearly everything she touched bombarded her senses if she wasn't careful. Though she'd successfully learned to control it over the years, her childhood had been challenging, to say the least. Even as an adult, when she was overwhelmed or distracted, as she was now, her carefully schooled defenses weren't entirely dependable. The gloves were her armor, and inquisitive looks were a small price to pay for insurance.

Weary, and sounding it even to her own ears, Tessa gave the driver her destination, wondering yet again why her father chose to spend his last days in a small hospital on the tiny boat shaped island in the middle of the river running through Rome. It would have made far more sense to stay in the small village up north that he'd called home for the last few years, where everyone knew and loved him. Or he could have come to stay with her in the States. Of course, the island had once been the site of an ancient temple to Aesculapius, the Greek god of medicine and healing, so maybe her father hadn't really given up all hope, but simply decided to cover all the bases. Putting his eggs in the basket of a pagan god was an odd choice for a former upper echelon angel, she thought. Apparently, even angels weren't above hedging their bets.

"*Certo, signorina,*" the driver replied, glancing at her in the mirror before returning his gaze to the meter. Finally, he shifted into gear and slowly nosed the small vehicle through the congested area around the international terminal and out onto the A91 in the direction of central Rome.

Thankfully, since she had neither the energy nor desire for polite small-talk, he kept silent except for occasionally blaring the horn and swearing loudly, and then murmuring an embarrassed '*mi scusi.*' Staring mostly at her feet and working hard to keep her thoughts away from what lay ahead, Tessa started when she looked out the window to see the Circus Maximus flashing by. The drive should have taken at least half an hour, yet it felt like only seconds passed. Heedless of her need to slow it down, time flew by on fast forward, sending her barreling ahead toward the unthinkable no matter how hard she dug in her heels and fought to stop the inevitable.

The cab turned to cross the river by way of *Ponte Garibaldi*, and the lights on the island became visible on her left. Her heart rate increased with every rotation of the tires, until it fluttered like a flock of sparrows fighting to free themselves from her ribcage. By the time the driver navigated the *Ponte Cestio* leading out to the island, her lungs screamed with the effort it took to breathe. She bit her lip, fighting the urge to direct the man to simply turn around and speed away from this place as fast as he could. Her father was in there and in all likelihood, he was never coming out. She did *not* want to deal with this. However, she didn't see any supernatural being standing around offering an alternative. She took a deep breath, handed the driver a pile of crumpled Euro she dug from the pocket of her jeans, and stepped out of the car, dragging her backpack behind her. Her father was dying. She could stand here denying the truth as much as she wanted, but failing to face facts never changed them.

Chapter Two

The automatic doors groaned in tired protest as Tessa impatiently shoved them aside and strode briskly to the information desk. Visiting hours were long past, the lobby dim and quiet at this time of night. The young woman behind the desk wore a huge quantity of blue-black hair teetering awkwardly on top of her head, and it looked heavy enough to snap her long, thin neck like a toothpick. Her nose was buried in a book, and she didn't bother to look up as she turned the page and announced visiting hours were over in a rehearsed tone of bored irritation.

"I know. *Mi dispiace*. I'm sorry, but I've only just arrived from the airport. I got here as quickly as I could. *Per favore*, I must see my father. He's…dying." Saying it out loud made it more real somehow, more definite, more…final. A knife twisted in her heart. How would she find the strength to say good-bye?

"Of course," the woman said in a kinder tone, setting the book on the desk after carefully marking her page, and poising her fingers over the computer keyboard. "*Come si chiamò?*"

"Bartolucci. His name is Eduardo Bartolucci," Tessa replied, providing her father's mortal name.

The woman tapped the keys and as the screen flickered and updated, her brows rose into her hairline and her expression softened. She spun in her chair toward Tessa and waved a manicured hand in the direction of the hallway on the right. "The elevator is just through there. Take it to the second floor and then use the stairs at the end of the hallway to go all the way to the top."

"*Grazie. Mille grazie.*" Tessa clutched her backpack to her chest like a shield against the coming pain, and hurried on boneless legs in the direction the receptionist indicated.

The elevator took an eternity to squeal and groan to the second floor, and Tessa breathed a sigh of relief when the doors finally slid open to reveal a nurse sitting at a desk, engrossed in paperwork. The woman looked up and nodded pleasantly, as Tessa offered a distracted smile and hurried to the stairwell at the end of the hall. When she finally pushed through the heavy door at the top, her chest ached and her leg muscles twitched in protest.

"*Buonasera.* Eduardo Bartolucci?"

"*Buonasera, signorina.* Down the hall and to the right, his is the last door on the left. He's waiting for you." The subtext was clear. He maintained his fragile grip on life to see her one last time and say good-bye. Tessa opened her mouth, but the words snagged in her throat, so she stiffly nodded her thanks and moved slowly in the direction of her father's room.

All of the prior urgency fell away and her limbs became leaden weights, refusing to move, as though her body hoped to stop time, while her mind screamed the inevitable rushed at her far too fast. She drew in a deep breath through her nose and slowly blew it out again through pursed lips. She had plenty of time to fall apart, to mourn, and to be alone. A lifetime, in fact. She blinked the moisture from her eyes and squared her shoulders. Her father sacrificed so much for her. She would not be selfish now, when it counted most. She could do this. She couldn't save him, but she could be strong and give him peace. He deserved it more than anyone she'd ever known.

****

"I thought there would be more time. As does everyone, I suppose." The pale figure in the bed opened his mouth as though he would say more, but a fit of coughing wracked the frail body, seizing his airway, leaving him wheezing and gasping for breath. After several minutes, he cleared his throat with a pained grimace and turned to fix his sunken eyes on Alec.

Alec swallowed thickly. He expected this would be difficult. The anticipation didn't even approach the reality. He planned to read Barachiel the riot act for putting him in this position. Then he intended to heap on a hefty portion of guilt for asking him to put his life on hold for a woman who'd walked away from their life together without a backward glance. Alec was the last person on the planet Tessa would seek comfort from at a time like this, and Barachiel must be well aware of that fact. The self-righteous anger smoldering in Alec's gut sputtered and died at the sight of the gaunt and wasted man lying in the bed. Eclipsed by life-sustaining tubes, wires, and machinery, the ancient one struggled to stay alert until his daughter arrived.

The words remained stuck in Alec's throat. He saw no resemblance in this poor soul to the mighty *Principalitie*, a prince of the heavens, who'd served mankind for millennia as educator, guardian, and muse. He saw a stranger—until the man turned to stare directly at him, and Alec looked into his eyes. They were eyes he remembered well, eyes that still shone with light, mischief, and centuries of remembered escapades despite the fragility of the pain plagued vessel which contained them. He told Michael he would recognize Barachiel's soul, and he did. Fresh grief sank a fist into Alec's middle, nearly doubling him over.

"I hoped for a stern lecture. Instead, you stand there sniveling like someone kicked your puppy. Don't grieve for me, Alec. While I admit, I'm sorry to leave, there is a part of me that's happy to be going home." He paused to draw in a rattling breath.

"Don't you dare tell me how to feel, you decrepit old man," Alec ground out through clenched teeth as his eyes flew open and his fingers curled into fists at his sides. "Damn you, you did this to yourself. You could have…" Sorrow clogged his throat and choked off the words. He dropped his chin to his chest and squeezed his eyes shut.

"I could have what? Lived forever? I will, you know. Not in this place and not in this form, but I will go on, Alec. We both know that. Only my time frame on earth changed. Well, and perhaps my stunning good looks. Not for the better I must admit," he wheezed out a hoarse chuckle. "Mortality is a bitch."

"Does she know? That you sent for me, I mean."

"You think I have a death wish?" He winked, smiling at his own bad joke. "Look, I know I'm asking a lot. And I'm grateful you came. I can go in peace knowing Tessa won't be alone through this."

For long moments, the rattle of the angel's dying breaths and the irregular bleeps of the heart monitor were the only sounds disturbing the peculiar stillness as those familiar eyes continued to bore into Alec. *Earthbound,* like Alec, were descended from angels redeemed after the Fall and tasked with battling the plots and schemes of the evil *Fallen* on Earth. They lived for centuries. *Principalitie,* like Barachiel, were true immortals. Or should have been. But, Barachiel gave up his heart and immortality for a beautiful Italian artist. When he learned she carried his child, he'd chosen a temporal life on Earth to remain with his family. Loss was as familiar to an *Earthbound* as breathing, and Alec was no stranger to the experience. Still, there was something fundamentally different about watching a powerful being slated for immortality reduced to a withered shell. Struggling, suffering, both fighting to live and fighting to die. It defied nature and he hated seeing the decline as the friend he loved traveled down that inexorable road.

He moved to the bed to grasp the dying man's fingers. They felt as light and fragile as a bird's skeleton in his hand, yet they gripped back with surprising strength.

"I should have kept in touch…"Alec began in a choked voice.

"I didn't ask you here for apologies and regret. You're here now when I need you. We were friends long before I became Contessa's father, and I vowed when the two of you fell in love I would remain a neutral party no matter what happened. Even when I thought you were a blind ass who spent his time searching for another man's treasure instead of appreciating the one right in front of his face. Even when I thought she behaved like a spoiled child and made the worst decision of her life. I kept my mouth shut and my opinions to myself."

"Well, I see you've decided to stop biting your tongue." Alec's lips curved upward. "Tell me how you really feel, why don't you?"

"Hey, divided loyalties are a bitch, you know?" He paused to draw in a rattling breath. "I'm old, Alec. Nearly as old as time itself. This mortal death is a small price to pay for the love of a beautiful woman and a child I thought never to have. The actual dying sucks, but this too shall pass. Don't grieve for me. Despite everything, I would make the same choices. No regrets. It was worth it."

"No regrets." Alec whispered, squeezing the older man's hand and knowing he lied to them both. He would always regret he failed to maintain this friendship, no matter what happened between him and Tessa. "I'm glad your choices brought you happiness."

"They did, but not without pain. Then again, without the pain, could we truly appreciate the joy? Maybe we aren't meant to have one without the other. But some things are worth any sacrifice." His eyes widened and then narrowed. "Help me up, Alec. I don't want to look frail and pathetic when my daughter arrives. This will be difficult enough for her as it is."

Alec's heart raced as he fumbled around the rail until he found the button to elevate the head of the bed. The knowledge Tessa drew ever nearer crept over his skin and something sparked to life, something deep and carefully buried. Slipping his arms under Barachiel's thin limbs, he lifted him gently and repositioned him, plumping the pillows behind his head, drawing the sheet to his waist, and folding it down neatly.

"Ah, much better. Thank you." Barachiel sighed

and his eyes fluttered closed. "How do I look?"

"Like shit." Alec couldn't suppress a small smile. *He was dying, how did he think he looked?* But he had to admit, his friend did look more comfortable, almost peaceful.

"Smartass," Barachiel returned the grin and opened one eye, fixing it intently on Alec. "Are you crying, you pathetic bastard?"

"Don't flatter yourself, you feeble sonofabitch." Alec swiped the back of his hand across his eyes. It felt disrespectful to indulge in their old ball-busting banter while staring death in the face, but if that's the way Barachiel wanted to play it, Alec wouldn't deny him. "They use enough bleach and disinfectant in this place to blind a person."

"Listen, I know this is a lot to ask. Try to remember she was young, idealistic. I sheltered her, kept her life conflict free right up until the day she married you." The dying man's sigh whistled and creaked in his chest. "I tried to give her the world, and instead cultivated immaturity and unrealistic expectations. Children should come with owners' manuals."

"Knock it off. You did say no regrets, remember? You were a wonderful father who gave her unconditional love, and she adores you. No one's perfect."

"Speak for yourself. She's also too stubborn for her own good, but then that's something the two of you have in common. She won't be happy I involved you."

"Ya think?" Alec's lips compressed into a tight line.

"It couldn't be helped. I've left some unfinished

business, and I need to know she'll be safe. I wish I had time to explain, but I have faith in you, Alec. I always have. Just remember, no matter what she's done, she's still the other half of you. And this, I think, is where we say good-bye," Barachiel rasped, closing his eyes.

"Rest easy, old friend." Alec cupped Barachiel's face in his hand, feeling the sharp jut of bone beneath the wrinkled tissue paper skin. Barachiel offered no response to this final touch, perhaps conserving his remaining strength for the emotional scene ahead. But, just as Alec withdrew his hand and stepped back from the bed, a single tear trickled from the outer corner of the old man's eye and disappeared into the wispy hair above his ear. With a strangled groan, Alec wrenched the door open and stumbled into the dimly lit hallway, blinded by sorrow, and having no specific destination in mind. He knuckled the moisture from his eyes and looked around. Michael had obviously left the building. Figured.

He needed distance, needed air. Dammit, how would he comfort a grieving estranged wife who didn't want him? Heaving a deep, shuddering sigh, he jogged down the hallway, turned the corner in the direction of the stairs, and crashed right into a woman with tousled red curls, thick, tear spiked lashes, and the most incredible blue eyes Alec ever saw. Eyes he never forgot.

****

Tessa swallowed the thick knot in her throat. *I can do this. I can do this. Dear God, how will I ever do this?* Eyes downcast, she turned the corner and promptly slammed into the unforgiving wall of a man's broad, muscular chest. Glancing up in surprise at his enormous height from beneath her damp lashes, she gasped at the six and a half feet of masculine perfection. Wide shoulders tapered to lean hips and long legs which he'd planted slightly apart as he simply stood there watching her with unblinking eyes. Her gaze traveled over the dark, tousled hair, the high cheekbones, and the sharply defined jaw dusted in a dark stubble falling somewhere between a well-trimmed beard and a five o'clock shadow. And good Lord, his eyes. Eyes flashing the deep blue of ocean waves in moonlight. Eyes in which she could easily drown. He hadn't changed. Alec McAllister was still the most beautiful man she'd ever seen.

Chapter Three

Alec instinctively reached out and gripped Tessa's shoulders to steady her as she gasped and stumbled back. She, in turn, curled her fingers into the front of his shirt to regain her balance.

"Alec. What are you doing here?"

"I came to see your father. You okay?" *Stupid question.*

"Yes, I'm fine." She drew in a deep breath, affording him a tantalizing glimpse of soft, white cleavage in the loose fitting neckline of her button-down blouse, as a becoming flush crept into her pale cheeks. She glanced up at him from under those thick lashes, loosened her death grip on his shirt, and tried to step away. It was only then Alec realized he still held her arms, his thumbs absently stroking the fabric covering her narrow shoulders.

"You can let go of me now," she whispered.

"Oh, yeah…sorry." He released her and took a half step back. She wore her thick, dark red hair piled in shining waves sitting haphazardly on top of her head, less a style than an afterthought, and he suddenly flashed back to its magnificence loose and spread across his pillow. *Damn.* He certainly had more important things to worry about at the moment. Still, it had been a long time, and his eyes greedily drank her in, making it difficult to look away. Her even, white teeth worried at her full bottom lip as she gripped the strap of her backpack and yanked it back into place when it slid down her shoulder.

"How did you know?"

"He contacted Michael."

"He contacted Michael?"

"Is there an echo in here?" Alec compressed his lips and shoved his hands into the front pockets of his jeans, curling his fingers into fists.

"Is that your lame attempt at humor? Please excuse me if I can't appreciate your sparkling wit at the moment." She surveyed him slowly from head to toe and back again. "I'm a little preoccupied."

"Of course you are." Alec sighed. "Look, we'll talk later. Go see your father. He's waiting for you."

What little color remained in her cheeks drained away, and she sucked in a deep, shuddering breath.

"I can't imagine what we'd have to talk about, but it was...good to see you, Alec. And thanks for coming by to see him. I'm sure it meant a lot. He always valued your friendship." She straightened her shoulders, stepped around him, and hurried down the hallway in the direction of Barachiel's room.

Alec retraced his footsteps, following slowly behind her, enjoying the sight of her gently rounded hips swaying slightly in the figure hugging denim and calling himself every kind of a fool for even noticing. He tried like hell to read her. But despite her grief, and the shock of seeing him, her mind remained closed as tight as a miser's purse, whether from habit or in preparation for the coming ordeal, he didn't know.

"Papa!" Alec heard the smile in her voice as she pushed open the door and slipped inside. He couldn't help admiring her courage. He'd seen the devastation in her eyes, yet she pulled herself together and mustered her strength before stepping into the room to allow her father a measure of peace in his passing.

"Contessa... *il mio più preziosa!*" Barachiel's labored rasp reached his ears as the door whooshed gently closed. "Come here, my precious one. There's much to say and little time in which to say it."

"Subtlety has never been your strong point, Sariel," Alec scrubbed a hand over the back of his neck as he reached the far end of the hall. He braced a shoulder against the wall, and quietly addressed the dark shadow lingering there. "You may as well show yourself."

The dark mass swirled and expanded, then shimmered and coalesced into the figure of a man. Dressed in black from head to toe, with dark hair and even darker eyes, he sported a massive set of golden wings that caught the light and surrounded him with an unearthly glow. Stepping forward, he gave them a mighty flap that ruffled Alec's hair, before settling them against his back where they neatly folded away out of sight in the blink of an eye.

"I thought my discretionary skills were improving." The dark angel frowned. "Perhaps not."

"Well, let's just say I expected you. I'd like to say it's nice to see you, but you know it never is."

"Frankly, I don't understand why. In the natural order of things, I'm the inevitable conclusion, Alec. My arrival offers peace and respite."

"Don't take it personally, buddy. I just don't think too many people enjoy getting up close and personal with the Angel of Death."

"I've always gotten a bum rap." Sariel's features

twisted in a grimace. "I don't *control* death, you know. I simply guide the soul over once it's passed."

"So you have nothing to do with the fact Eduardo Bartolucci managed to linger hours longer than his body could support life? I saw him, Sariel. No amount of determination to say good-bye to his daughter should have been able to sustain him."

"I'm willing to take the heat if we're a little late getting home. It's Barachiel, after all." The dark angel shrugged.

"Thank you."

"Save your thanks, I didn't do it for you. I did it for her." He jerked his thumb in the direction of Barachiel's room and his lips curled in a small, secretive smile. "By the way, good luck with that. And now, if you'll excuse me, it's nearly time."

Before Alec could open his mouth to say another word, the angel dissipated into thin air. Alec's phone vibrated in his pocket, and he yanked it free, glancing down to see his brother-in-law Luca's name on the display. His stomach dropped into his boots as the dark shadow slipped by him and disappeared under the door to Barachiel's room as he brought the phone to his ear.

"Congratulate me, Alec! The doctor says your sister is going to give me a beautiful daughter!"

"Congratulations," Alec responded automatically, knowing it had to be the wee hours of the morning in New York. Listening with only half an ear as Luca waxed poetic for endless minutes about the ultrasound revealing what he assured Alec was the most beautiful child who would ever be born, Alec's gaze never strayed from the door to Barachiel's room. Of course his niece would be beautiful. Luca was a great looking guy as guys go, and Alec's sister, Callista, was a true beauty. Alec participated absently in the conversation with an occasional grunt until Tessa, eyes red-rimmed and swollen, slipped from the room and slumped against the wall. "Hey, buddy, give Calli my love, okay? Gotta go."

"But—" Luca's voice was cut off mid-sentence as Alec tapped the screen and shoved the phone back in his pocket, stepping toward Tessa. Resisting the almost primal urge to touch her, he fisted his hands, shifting his weight from one foot to the other. Seemingly oblivious to his presence, slender hands covering her face, her shoulders shook with quiet sobs. Small and sad, she looked more alone than anyone Alec ever saw, and something twisted painfully in the region of his heart. Anger and resentment aside, this woman still touched him in a place no one else ever had, nor ever would.

He thought of Luca's call. How intertwined were happiness and grief. One soul preparing to enter the world as another departs. Sariel called it the natural order. *Screw that shit.* Dragging his hands free, he reached out and pulled Tessa into his arms.

She stiffened at first, flattening her hands against his chest as though she would push him away. Then she sagged against him with a shuddering sob and wrapped her arms around his waist. Alec lost track of time as he held her, her heartbroken tears soaking his chest while her hands bunched and twisted his shirt at the small of his back. Knowing there were no words, he rested his cheek on the top of her head, breathing in her familiar raspberry scent, and curled his body protectively around hers. Then he simply let her cry until her tears were spent. When her grip on his shirt finally eased and her heart-wrenching sobs subsided to sad little hiccoughs, Alec pulled back slightly, and looked down into her tear-mottled face.

"We should go," he said gently, rubbing his hands up and down the length of her back.

"Go? But aren't there arrangements...don't I have to sign papers or something?" She gazed up at him with a lost expression.

"That's all been taken care of. Your father didn't want any fuss when he..." Despite his best effort, Alec's voice broke. He knew his pain couldn't compare with hers, and maybe all things considered he didn't even have the right to grieve, but he felt the ache of loss nonetheless. He roughly cleared his throat. "The Brothers who oversee the hospital will take care of everything. It's why he came here. It's what they do when one of us...moves on. Actually, in the mortal world, this floor doesn't even exist."

"I see," she whispered, her eyes welling again. "So that's it, then. It's all over and he's just...gone. And he appointed *you* my own personal go-to guy. And you agreed? What in the hell am I supposed to do with *that*?"

"We'll talk about it later. I know it doesn't feel like it at the moment, but he'll never be further away than the best memories you hold in your heart. And I know you have tons of those."

She nodded, blinking rapidly. "I know. It's not quite the same though, is it?"

"No, it's not the same," Alec agreed. "If it helps at all, even though your father inspired some of the greatest art and literature in the history of the world, in the thousands of years of his existence, he considered *you* his greatest accomplishment. You brought him his greatest joy."

"Thank you." After a moment, to his surprise, she chuckled and swiped the back of her hand across her eyes. "He must have led a sadly boring existence if I was the highlight."

"Hardly," Alec grinned in return. "Remind me to tell you about our sojourn in sixteenth century Paris sometime. Now, are you ready?"

"I can't really imagine any circumstances under which we'd be having that conversation, Alec. But, thank you again for coming to see him at the end. Really. I know it meant a lot to him."

"I loved him, too."

Tessa pressed her lips together, dropped her chin to her chest, and nodded. Then she drew in a deep breath and stretched her long neck, sending the remnants of her poorly constructed up-do tumbling around her shoulders like russet silk against the snowy background of her blouse. Alec bit back a groan as his blood rushed to a location it had no business seeking out under the circumstances. Or any circumstances. *Damn.*

"I suppose I should call for a taxi. My father leased a place in the *Borgo* and moved our things there when he became ill. I have the address here somewhere." As if she'd only just realized she was still standing in his arms, she stepped back unsteadily and dug in her pocket. Alec dropped his arms to his sides, immediately feeling the loss of her warmth. Fighting the urge to drag her back against him, he bent and retrieved her backpack where she'd dropped it and slung it over his shoulder.

"We'll check out the place later. Right now, you're coming home with me, and you don't need a cab."

****

Tessa's alarmed gaze flew to his face He looked completely serious. Okay, so maybe earlier she'd wished for someone to hold her, someone to comfort her and share the unfathomable sense of loss. At a moment when she'd needed someone most, Alec certainly seemed like the answer to a prayer. The person she most wanted, but least expected. Still, at the end of the day, no matter how compassionate he appeared, no matter what they'd been to one another, and no matter what her father said, she sure as hell wasn't going home, or anywhere else, with him. That couldn't end well. At all.

"Um…I don't think so, but thank you," She yanked her gloves from the back pocket of her jeans and tugged them on. Then, she reached out and curled her fingers around the strap of her backpack where it rested along his shoulder. "Will you please give me my things?"

"What? Oh sure, sorry." He casually shrugged free of the strap, and she stumbled back against the wall, heart pounding, and holding the bag against her chest like a shield.

"Look, I know my father asked you to give me a hand getting things sorted out and to look out for me, but you know he's always been overprotective. And given our history…well, it's probably not the best idea, you know? I'll miss him terribly of course, but I'll be fine. People do this every day, right? I appreciate the invitation, but I'll be going to the flat just as I planned." Exhausted, empty, and lacking the strength to deal with her estranged husband, what she wanted most was to curl up in a ball and cry until the panicked ache clawing insistently at the inside of her chest began to ease. Her father was gone. "Consider yourself off the hook."

"Here's the problem. You're apparently under the impression I was issuing an invitation, or that I'm giving you a choice. You need sleep and some good old-fashioned coddling. In short, you need my mother."

Before Tessa could formulate a reply, he leaned forward and pulled her back into his arms. She had a single heartbeat to appreciate the solid strength of him and then the world spun away.

Chapter Four

"How *dare* you?" Tessa sputtered, first stumbling, and then shoving hard against him, as they reformed moments later in the back garden of his mother's home on *Via Dandolo*. She twisted away, nostrils flaring, and stood facing him with her feet shoulder-width apart and hands fisted at her sides.

"How dare I bring you to a place where you can relax in safety and be taken care of? Oh, I don't know, I guess I'm just an inconsiderate jerk."

The first orange fingers of dawn creeping out to tickle the wispy streaks of gray stretching along the horizon provided just enough light to discern the dangerous spark in her eyes. Alec could live with angry. It allowed him to keep his own anger near the surface, and bury other less welcome emotions determined to bubble up whenever she was near. Yeah, royally pissed was preferable to desolate and inconsolable any day of the week as far as he was concerned.

"That wasn't fair!"

"I don't have to be fair," Alec replied. "This isn't a democracy, you know."

"You can't just go around doing things like that to people without warning," she whispered in a tremulous voice, and only then did Alec realize she was trembling from head to toe. *Well, shit.*

"Tessa..." he stepped toward her and held out a hand.

"Don't you touch me," she warned, taking a quick step back, eyeing him warily.

Okay, so maybe he'd been an oblivious jackass. Hardly the first time, but maybe it showed progress if he'd noticed without someone else pointing it out?

"Look, I could have warned you, but frankly it just never occurred to me. You've had a long night, and you're tired and hurting. I get it. I'm not happy about this, but believe it or not, I really am trying to help. I'm not the bad guy here."

"Meaning I am?" She spat, stepping right up toe to toe, crossing her arms over her chest, and craning her neck to look directly into his face. "I fly thousands of miles, watch my father die, and then, before I can even process what that means, I am grabbed by *you*, of all people, and spirited off against my will without so much as a by-your-leave. And you have the audacity to stand there and tell me *you're* not happy about this?"

Alec decided he definitely preferred angry Tessa. Her eyes deepened to the swirling blue of an angry sea and her chest heaved, straining the buttons of the wrinkled white blouse and thrusting her high breasts against the thin fabric. With her bright eyes snapping, red-gold curls tumbling over her shoulders, and her cheeks hot and flushed, pissed or not, she was freakin' magnificent.

"Okay, let's agree neither of us are happy about this. You're still staying here."

"You're impossible!" She threw up her hands in the universal gesture for frustration and bent to retrieve her backpack while mumbling under her breath in rapid

Italian. Glancing around wildly, she turned and stomped toward the walkway leading to the front of the villa. He caught up to her in two long strides and grasped her upper arm, spinning her to face him. She struggled automatically, stopping short as a woman's voice floated out of the back door into the still morning air.

"Alec, if you've finished badgering the poor girl, the coffee is on the table."

"Who's that?" Tessa whispered in a shaky voice.

"I realize it's been a while, but surely you haven't forgotten my mother?"

"*Madge*? You were serious? You're living with your mother?"

"No, but you know I stay with her when I'm in Rome." Alec shrugged. "Is that a problem?"

"No…no, of course not. It's just that I thought…oh, never mind."

"You thought what? That I brought you here to… Well, sweetness, sorry to disappoint you, but even *I'm* not that insensitive. Or desperate."

"You flatter yourself. I'm not disappointed in the least. Self-centered, overbearing mama's boys aren't my type."

Alec reminded himself she'd just lost her father, and bit back the sharp retort that sprang automatically to his lips. He settled for following slowly behind as Tessa shook off his hand and marched back to the kitchen door, climbing the stairs right into Magdalena McAllister's open arms.

"I'm so sorry about your father, my dear," Madge murmured quietly. "We loved him, too." Tessa nodded into the other woman's shoulder, but if she responded, she kept her voice too low for Alec to hear.

"Don't take it personally, darling. The girl is grieving." His mother's amused voice entered his mind through the telepathic channel used by his family.

"Exactly whose side are you on, Mother?" Alec sent the disgruntled reply.

"I didn't know we were engaged in a battle, dear. Now come in and sit down. It's been a long night."

"How did you know?" Alec asked as he pulled out a chair across the table from Tessa and dropped his tired ass on it.

"Michael stopped by earlier," his mother explained vaguely, setting steaming mugs of coffee in front of them before resuming her own seat. Tessa smiled her thanks, extended a hand for her cup, then hesitated, as Madge arched a manicured brow at her gloved hands.

"Sorry, forgot," Tessa mumbled as a lovely apricot stained her cheeks. She peeled her gloves off and stuffed them in her pocket. "When I'm distracted the gloves afford me the freedom to concentrate on other things and avoid getting smacked with an unexpected vision."

"I've always found your gift fascinating," Madge brought her cup to her lips, regarding Alec steadily over the rim, and took a sip. "Psychometry is rare, even among our kind. Your father always claimed it both a handy talent to have and a terrible curse to bear. Depending on the circumstances, of course. I expect it's much the same for you." Setting her cup back on the table, she turned her full attention to Tessa with a smile. "You must be exhausted. Finish your coffee and I'll show you up to one of the guest rooms."

"That's very kind of you, Madge." Tessa pushed

the cup away and rose to her feet, glancing covertly at Alec. "But as I tried to tell your son, my father arranged a place for me to stay."

"Nonsense," Madge waved her off. "I will not have you going off alone, especially at a time like this. Besides, if your father really intended for you to stay there alone, he would never have arranged for Alec to fetch you. Now come along, young lady. Let's get you settled in. I'm sure we can find something to fit you."

"But…"

Alec relaxed back in his chair with a grin and stretched his legs out in front of him, ignoring the desperate glances Tessa aimed in his direction. His mother operated like a rip tide, and he'd learned long ago it was much easier to go with her flow than swim against the current. He'd counted on her taking charge of the situation for the night. Not only was she a much better caretaker than he could ever hope to be, Tessa had always been fond of her and would no doubt find more comfort in his mother's company than his.

"Don't tell me you forgot my mother is an old cat lady. Except instead of stray cats, she collects people. Resistance is futile. It's best to save your energy, submit willingly, and try to get some rest."

"I don't understand. Neither of you has the slightest reason to be kind to me," Tessa shook her head and whispered quietly as moisture gathered in her eyes.

"We McAllisters take care of our own," Madge said by way of explanation. Coming around the table, she wrapped an arm around Tessa's slim shoulders and steered her toward the doorway leading to the parlor and the stairs beyond.

"We can go to the apartment later, if you like. You

can see what's there, decide what you want to keep, and I'll arrange to have it moved here temporarily until I decide what to do," Alec offered. Tessa stiffened against his mother's side and skidded to a stop, before turning back to him with wide eyes and flaming cheeks.

"I'm sorry? Did you say until *you* decide what to do? I'm sure I heard you wrong because I don't recall giving you authority to make my decisions for me. My father may have appointed you my trusty guardian, but I didn't. I'm quite capable of looking after myself, and *I* didn't agree to anything," Tessa ground out through clenched teeth.

"You do recall this isn't a democracy, right?" Alec pressed his lips into a thin line. He was doing his best to accommodate a woman who'd thrown his heart in his face and walked out on him...for another man. She really could show a little gratitude. Or at least a modicum of polite appreciation. Most people considered him the easy-going McAllister. When had he turned into such a controlling bastard? He swallowed hard as he realized his sudden need to flex his macho directly correlated to the moment Tessa barreled into his chest and back into his life, gazing up at him with those wide, blue eyes and tear spiked lashes.

"Look," Alec pinched the bridge of his nose between his thumb and forefinger and looked up through his lashes with a sigh. The purple smudges beneath Tessa's eyes and the fragile pallor remaining once the angry flush drained from her cheeks struck him like a fist to the gut. "I didn't mean that exactly the way it sounded. It's been a hell of a night, yeah? We'll figure it all out after you've had some rest."

"Yeah, it *has* been a hell of a night." She regarded

him steadily before turning her attention back to his mother with a wan smile. "But it's no excuse for rudeness. It's poor repayment for your kind hospitality, Madge. I apologize. To you."

"Don't be silly. You have nothing to apologize for. Alec is a typical McAllister male. Don't hold it against him. I do believe it's genetic. On his father's side, of course." His mother gave him a pointed look that made Alec want to stick out his tongue. He settled for an exaggerated eye roll instead.

"While you, my darling mother, are ever docile and accommodating," Alec snorted.

"Well, I agree a congenital defect is clearly beyond his control." Tessa offered Madge a somber expression. "I'll try to remember that the next time he assumes I haven't a brain in my head."

"Hey, wait a minute! I didn't…" Alec straightened in his chair and started to protest he'd never assumed any such thing, when he saw the corner of her lips twitch. Was she teasing him? It touched something deep inside that despite all she'd suffered in the last few hours, she could overlook his awkward attempt to play protector and find some humor in it. His lips curled in return. "Okay, maybe I did throw myself into the saddle of my high horse with a little more enthusiasm than necessary. But understand this, Contessa. No matter how you feel about it, no matter how I feel about it, I made your father a promise and I intend to keep it."

"In that case, while I appreciate your commitment, I feel compelled to point out your implementation needs work." Her small, white teeth sank into her full bottom lip. "A lot of work."

Then she turned and followed his mother out of the

room without another word, leaving Alec at the kitchen table with his mouth hanging open.

****

Madge McAllister bustled around the room closing the wooden shutters against the rising sun, after handing Tessa a thin cotton nightie pulled from an antique mahogany chest of drawers just inside the door of the large, airy bedroom. Tessa quickly stripped out of the wrinkled traveling clothes that stuck to her skin as though she'd been wearing them for weeks instead of hours. Inhaling the fresh, clean scent of sun dried cotton, she let the lightweight sleepwear drop over her head, tugged the hem down to her knees, and climbed into the big bed Madge turned down for her. The plush mattress enveloped her in a welcoming embrace and a little of the tension of the last few hours eased.

"Can I get you anything else, dear?" Madge asked as she paused near the door.

"No, thank you," Tessa said in a choked voice. "You've already done so much…I don't know what to say. Thank you hardly seems adequate."

"I told you, we take care of our own," the older woman smiled.

"I guess I'm surprised you still feel I fall into that category," Tessa sighed. "Of all people, I thought you'd be the last one feeling charitable where I was concerned. I never intended—well, you know what they say about the best intentions. I *am* sorry I hurt him, you know. Nothing turned out the way I planned."

"I think maybe it's more accurate to say you hurt each other. I love my children with every breath in my body, Tessa, but I recognize they aren't perfect. No one is. No one knows what truly goes on in a marriage aside from the two people involved, and there are always three sides—his, hers, and the truth. Get some rest, child," Madge crossed to the bed and pressed her lips to Tessa's forehead before she withdrew, leaving her alone with her grief and her thoughts. Tessa pulled the sheet to her chin, and stared dry-eyed at the ceiling's ornate plaster work. She always believed visitation hours and funerals were barbaric rituals, but now with her father simply gone, she almost longed for the comfort of tradition and the blessed occupation of mind provided by preparations and logistics. Now she understood. The customs existed to bring comfort to the living, diversions designed to ease the heart with a respite from the reality. Flowers and tears were for the living. They were useless to the dead.

Now finally alone, the grief enveloping her felt too deep for tears. They'd been replaced by a persistent ache in her chest and the hollow nausea of a swift kick in the gut. Neither felt as though they'd be going away anytime soon. Abandoning her contemplation of the plaster rosettes, Tessa rolled to her side, found a cool spot in the bed, and pulled her knees into her chest, curling in a tight, tense ball. Her father supported her decision to leave Alec. Then again, her father supported every decision she ever made, whether he agreed with it or not. But as he lay dying, he'd shoved her right back into Alec's life. After all these years, was this his way of telling her he thought she'd made a mistake? Or was it simply her father's final gift, a familiar face so she didn't have to navigate this alone? Fragile was scary and unfamiliar territory. Maybe it was okay to let someone else worry about the bogeymen for a little while? At least until she resolved this desperate sensation of being a glass figure about to shatter into a million pieces. Whatever her father's reasons, she couldn't deny Alec's arms provided comfort when she needed it most. Ten years ago, her desperate ploy for attention blew up in her face. Alec had neither forgotten nor forgiven. This time, this transition, could only be a temporary respite, at best.

Chapter Five

Alec stared at the bottom of his coffee cup, as if he might find answers in the dregs. *She betrayed me. So why can she still tie me in knots?*

"Tessa looks well," Alec's mother remarked as she re-entered the kitchen and resumed her place at the table across from him. She reached for her cooling coffee and took a long, thoughtful sip before setting the cup back on the table and regarding him intently.

"I guess," Alec responded with a shrug. If he pretended disinterest, maybe he'd get there—eventually. *Fake it until you make it.*

"Uh-huh."

"Don't hold your breath thinking this means more than it does. It's a favor for a friend. I'm quite happy as I am."

"Are you really?"

"Sure. I come and go as I please, answer to no one. Hell, I don't even keep a permanent residence." Why should he? No matter how many women offered to share his bed, none stirred his interest. Only one ever had, or ever would, own his heart. Each set of rooms was as empty as another. Only the view out the window changed.

"Have you given any thought to what you'll do when Michael no longer requires your services?"

Alec slowly straightened in his chair as his eyes

widened and an invisible hand seized his throat making it difficult to suck in a breath.

"Exactly what did Michael tell you when he stopped by earlier?"

Madge's lips compressed in a thin line. Her chair screeched against the weathered floor tiles as she pushed it back and rose to her feet. Gathering up both her cup and Tessa's, she stepped to the sink and deposited them. Gripping the edge of the marble counter, her shoulders rose beneath the silk dressing robe as she drew in a deep breath and blew it out again, before turning to regard her son from beneath lowered brows.

"He simply confirmed what I'd more or less figured out for myself quite some time ago. It may have escaped your notice, but I've been around for well over a thousand years. I'm not blind, you know."

"If you knew I was working for Michael, why didn't you ever say anything?" Alec grumbled, wondering exactly how much his mother actually did see.

"Why didn't you ever tell me?" His mother shot back, lifting her chin as though preparing for a fight. "Tessa knew."

"Of course, she did. But, aside from sharing it with her, Michael swore me to secrecy, though apparently that oath doesn't extend to him. Besides, I figured you had enough on your plate."

"You may find this difficult to believe, but I've resigned myself to the fact my children are adults with several hundred years of life experience under their belts. I try very hard to keep my fears and my opinions to myself and not offer unsolicited advice."

Alec snorted and made no effort to hide his skeptical expression. Which she pointedly ignored.

"The fact is, I'm a mother. I will *always* worry. I worry about each one of you every single time you're out of my sight. It doesn't really matter whether you're out hunting *Fallen* in a dark alley, or researching a paper trail of lost objects in some dusty library, or even doing something as innocent as eating pickles and ice cream while your unborn baby kicks you in the ribs. When you're happy, I'm happy. When you're miserable, my heart breaks. When you look at yourself in the mirror, you see a grown man. When I look at you? I still see a small boy with a runny nose and skinned knees. A little boy I could keep safe from the world. A little boy who needed me."

"Aw, Mom…" Alec rose from the chair and stepped across the kitchen to wrap his arms around his mother, shocked to feel her trembling. Madge McAllister was a rock. Even when her husband was killed in battle. Even when faced with the death of her only daughter at the hands of a psychotic killer. She kept it together, she comforted others, she put one foot in front of the other without ever seeming to stumble. Of course, given enough time, and battered by a hostile environment, he supposed even bedrock could crumble.

"I'll always need you, silly woman. But I'm pretty capable of wiping my own nose these days," he murmured into her hair.

"Well, at least there are some advantages to you growing up," she sniffed with a laugh. She stepped back and swiped a forefinger under her eyes. "The work you're doing for Michael may be important, but ultimately it's his problem, not yours."

"McAllisters have always been fighters, I just use books instead of a blade."

"I see." The skeptical expression on her face didn't match her words.

"It needs to be done." Alec shrugged uncomfortably. His mother had always been a tad too perceptive, especially where her children were concerned. "And I'm good at it."

"I don't doubt that for an instant, but I suspect this quest to recover all of Michael's little indiscretions has cost you far more than it's given you in return. Maybe it's time to consider what makes *you* truly happy. Just promise me you'll never forget being *Earthbound* doesn't make you indestructible, it makes you a target."

"Where's this coming from all of a sudden?" Alec took a large sip of coffee to allow his mother a moment to regain her usual degree of composure. In truth, he needed a moment to regain his own. It had been the most bizarre twenty-four hours he remembered in a long time. First Barachiel's death, then Tessa barreling back into his life, and now this unexpected and out of character heart to heart with his mother. Overall, he felt like he'd been hit by a truck.

His mother glanced toward the door and back. Then she shrugged.

"I don't know. I guess maybe Barachiel's death has me contemplating the fleeting nature of life. Even ours. No matter how long we live, it's too short a time to spend it being unhappy. And seeing Tessa again, and the way you look at her, I guess I just remembered a time…"

"I'm perfectly content with my life, Mother," he interrupted shortly. As long as he didn't stop and think about it too much. "Don't forget, she's the one who left, not me. Tell me, do you subject my sainted brother to these enlightening lectures?"

"Not word for word, but yes. Several times over the years, in fact. Especially after your sister disappeared and he insisted on assuming the responsibility for something that was never his fault. Of course, now it's Katrina's job to keep him in line, thank the saints. I needed the break."

"Well, I would say she has her work cut out for her, but it's nearly impossible to pull one over on an empath. Between that and the fact he adores her, I think maybe she's got the upper hand." Alec smirked.

"I think maybe she does," his mother agreed "Although I *would* think twice about saying so to your brother who still harbors the delusion he's in charge."

"He hasn't been in charge since the day he met her," Alec laughed. "He just won't admit it. I wasn't sure anyone could save him from himself. But Kat did. I'll always be grateful to her for that."

"Maybe he was finally ready to be saved." Madge smiled. "But, you're right. I'm grateful, too. It does my heart good to know your brother finally has his priorities in order "

"Meaning I don't?"

"I'm not sure what yours are. Now, you should probably go and try to get some sleep, too. If the exchange I overheard between you and Contessa in the garden earlier is any indication, I have a feeling you're going to need it."

"The situation will be a lot easier to deal with once she's had some rest." Alec ran a hand through his hair and indulged in a jaw cracking yawn.

"She's heartbroken and exhausted. She isn't a situation, she's a woman with feelings and opinions. The sooner you get that through your head, the better."

"I'm well aware she's a woman, Mother," he grumbled irritably. "No worries on that score. And trust me, she can hold her own."

"There's still a spark between you." A statement, not a question.

"There will always be a 'spark', as you so eloquently put it. You know how it works, Mother. We're not just married, we're bound mates. Two halves of the same soul. I think we've conclusively proven even that doesn't guarantee happily-ever-after."

"Maybe. Maybe not." Madge pushed him in the direction of the door. "Get some sleep. I'm meeting some friends at the new Caravaggio exhibit at the *Galleria Borghese* after lunch, and then I have dinner plans, so I may not be here when you wake up. Maria will be in later and I'll have her leave something for you and Tessa in case you're hungry and don't want to go out."

"Okay," he yawned, heading for the stairs. "Be careful."

"Always am."

"And Mom?" He stopped in the doorway without turning around. "I may not say it very often, but I do love you, you know. You're the best."

"I am, aren't I?" He couldn't miss smile in her voice. "I love you, too, my baby boy. I love you, too."

Alec climbed the stairs slowly, the heavy stiffness in his limbs reminding him he hadn't slept in nearly forty-eight hours. Some vacation *this* turned out to be. He'd need two weeks at an all-inclusive in the

Caribbean to recover from it at this rate. Hauling himself to the top of the stairs, he totally intended to turn to the right in the direction of his own room. *Totally.* But his feet, it seemed, had a mind of their own and before he even thought about it, he found himself at the opposite end of the hall standing outside of the heavy wooden door of the room his sister used when she came to Rome. Maybe he'd been a little rough on Tessa earlier, but he'd been knocked for a loop by the mere sight of her. Still, she had just been through one of the worst nights of her life, so maybe he owed her an apology of sorts. He sucked in a deep whistling breath and blew it out slowly before rapping lightly on the door.

He no sooner let out a sigh of relief at the lack of response to his tentative knock when a soft, sleep thickened voice called out.

"Come in."

Alec swiped his sweat slicked palms down the side of his jeans, turned the knob, and cracked open the door. With her fiery locks tumbled around her face in tangled disarray, Tessa huddled in the center of the bed, sheet clutched to her breasts. The neckline of the thin, white nightgown slipped off to the side revealing a tantalizing glimpse of creamy shoulder. Her blue eyes were heavy-lidded and drowsy, and Alec experienced a vivid memory of her waking up in his arms after a night of passion. Then it hit him. She'd chosen someone else. That thought diverted the blood pounding into his groin right back into his general circulation.

"Sorry, didn't mean to wake you," he muttered in a strained voice, annoyed at his body's instantaneous reaction to the sight of her. He started to close the door.

"No, wait. It's okay...I wasn't really sleeping anyway." She flushed and tugged at her neckline until her shoulder was hidden from view. Shoving her heavy mass of hair away from her face, she wriggled until she was sitting completely upright. "Did you want something?"

Damn straight he wanted something, but that was his libido talking, not his common sense. He slipped quickly through the door and dropped hard into a Seventeenth Century arm-chair upholstered in the Turkey work fabric popular at the time, scooting it up next to the bed. Snatching a small, decorative pillow from the pile near the headboard, he shoved it behind his aching neck, holding his breath as the ancient wood creaked and groaned under his weight and careless mistreatment. Thankfully, the thing remained in one piece.

"Listen I, uh..." Alec shifted in the chair. "I acted like a jerk earlier. I was so busy concentrating on my own stuff, and how I felt, I didn't consider what any of this must be like for you. I know how much you loved your father, and how much you'll miss him. You sure as hell didn't need my attitude on top of it. So, for what it's worth, I'm sorry."

"I'm sorry, too," Tessa sighed. "I was tired and sad and scared. Angry at myself I wasn't here sooner. I still don't understand how it all happened so quickly. Frankly, I was completely shocked to see you."

"Probably about as shocked as I was to be seen. Tell you what," he sat forward and reached out a hand. "Let's try this again, shall we? Hello, Tessa. It's good to see you. I'm really not a complete ass most of the time."

She gripped his hand in her much smaller, softer one and smiled faintly.

"Hello, Alec. You have your moments. It's good to see you, too, and I'm really not an argumentative shrew most of the time."

"You have your moments. Well, now we've gotten that out of the way, I guess I should go and hit the sack and let you get some rest, too. We'll talk later." He reluctantly withdrew his hand from the silken warmth of hers. Her fingers tightened convulsively around his before she released him.

"Actually, I, uh, had one of my nightmares. I wouldn't mind something to distract me for a bit."

Alec raised a brow.

"I meant maybe we could talk," she clarified with a frown. "If you aren't too tired, that is. I don't imagine you've gotten any more sleep than I have in the last twenty-four hours."

"Talk. Yeah, sure. I'm not tired. Nope, not at all," he lied, thinking it had been well *over* twenty-four hours since he'd last seen the back of his eyelids.

He slouched down and settled more comfortably into the chair, as comfortably as a man his size could manage in a chair intended for someone much smaller and lighter, and propped his booted feet on the mattress. Tessa turned on her side to face him and snuggled down into the bed regarding him intently, then offered him another faint smile.

"You were never a very good liar, Alec. You're exhausted. Go to bed. The nightmares are nothing new, I should be used to them. Residual stress. The worst has already happened, right?"

"Yeah, the worst has already happened." At least

he hoped to hell it had. Why should she be having nightmares now after her father was already dead? Oh well, not his problem anymore. Maybe she was right and it was nothing more than an emotional hangover. "What do you want to talk about?"

"Oh, I don't know." She hesitated. "A divorce?"

Chapter Six

Tessa white-knuckled the bedclothes and pulled them to her throat as Alec's boots hit the floor with the force of a shotgun blast. He jerked upright in the chair and leaned forward, pinning her to the bed with his gaze.

"You filed for divorce?" he ground out through stiff lips.

"No, I, uh…oh, hell, Alec, it's been ten years." Tessa sighed and pushed herself back into a seated position. "Maybe it's time to cut our losses and move on."

"Cut our losses," he echoed, easing back against the chair and crossing his arms over his chest. "I'm not the one who threw away the moon to run off and chase the stars. That was all *you*."

"A person doesn't have to be physically absent to throw away the moon and chase stars, you know."

"No." He'd run naked through Hell doused in gasoline before he agreed.

"No?"

"No, I won't give you a divorce."

"I wasn't asking for one, I was offering. I thought, after all these years, maybe you… maybe you found someone else—"

"As I recall, that's your modus operandi, sweetness, not mine."

"I guess you think I deserve that," she whispered, her eyes searching his face.

"Damn straight you do," Alec snapped, shoving back the chair and rising to his feet. "But hey, it isn't all on you. I took you for granted, became obsessed with the work. Isn't that what you said? I get it now. Of course, maybe if I'd been a *Defensori* like my brother, or some other larger than life hero, I would have been enough. I guess the pen really isn't mightier than the sword, no matter how skillfully it's wielded, is it?"

"I never needed a hero, Alec. Only a husband." Tessa gasped, wincing as though he'd slapped her, and sank back against the pillows. "You thought you weren't enough?"

"My opinion of myself is just fine, thanks. And yours doesn't matter, anymore."

Dear God, Tessa thought, as her heart contracted into a cold, painful lump. *What have I done?*

He crossed his arms over his chest, hands curled into tight fists, and turned his face away toward the window. He clenched his jaw so tightly, its sharp angles appeared carved in stone.

In her childish desperation to be the acknowledged center of his universe, she'd not only broken two hearts and destroyed a marriage, she'd caused him to doubt himself, doubt his worth. Yes, he'd been a blind fool. He owned part of the blame. But, she'd taken a difficult situation and made it worse. Well, she might deserve to pay the price for her foolishness for the remainder of her very long life, but Alec did not.

"Alec, there's something I should tell you," Tessa croaked, twisting her fingers together in her lap and clearing her throat. Alec didn't so much as flick his eyes in her direction. He simply continued to stare at the wall as though she hadn't spoken. "You're probably going to be angry…" If possible, his jaw clenched even tighter and his lips thinned. "Um, okay, so you're already angry. Well, I had a plan, you see, but somehow it all went wrong. I never meant for it to go so far. I didn't know how to…I should have told you—"

"There's only one thing I need you to tell me, Tessa," Alec ground out, turning back to face her. His hands dropped to his sides, but remained tightly clenched. His pain filled eyes, two bottomless pools darkened nearly to black, pinned her to the bed, stabbing sharply at her conscience. "His name. Give me the bastard's name."

****

Alec cracked open his eyelids with a groan, shifting his weight on the hard antique settee that hadn't even been designed for fleeting comfort let alone sleeping. After storming from Tessa's room when she declined to identify the sonofabitch, he headed straight for the library. He grabbed the first bottle that came to hand, well aware it would take a hell of a lot more than a good stiff drink to ease the memory of his own failures and the ache of her infidelity in his heart. But, even though alcohol had little effect on an *Earthbound*, three bottles of Scotch, combined with the emotional toll of the last twenty-four hours and a significant lack of sleep, actually managed to produce a slight buzz. What difference did learning the bastard's identity make now? Knowing would probably only sharpen the sting. Still, the thought of finding himself in the same room with the guy and being ignorant of it…well, he didn't much like that idea, either. He'd only intended to close his eyes for a moment before heading to his own bed, but somehow he managed to doze off.

A quick glance at his watch told him it was just after three. He scrubbed a hand over his stubble roughened jaw, before hauling himself to his feet. A coverlet tucked in around him twisted about his legs and foiled his attempt to get upright. How many times did he fall asleep at his desk, his nose buried in some dusty research, never having made it to their bed, only to wake up tucked in snugly by Tessa? Too often, probably. Well, it was a sure bet she didn't tuck him in this time.

He took the stairs two at a time, and rapped sharply on her door. Receiving no response, he cracked it open and found the room empty and the bed neatly made. He showered and dressed in record time, and then headed back downstairs to find Tessa. He'd promised to take her to the flat today, though he knew it would be difficult for her. He certainly didn't look forward to it. She'd need comfort, and even though she allowed him to provide it last night, he probably made damn sure she wouldn't want him anywhere near her today. Entering the kitchen, he found his mother's housekeeper, Maria, humming over an enormous pot she stirred on the stove. The rich herbed tomato and beef scented steam rising from the soup filled the kitchen. The table was cleared, the sink was empty, and there was no sign of Tessa.

"Morning, Maria." He grabbed an apple from the wooden bowl on the counter and sank his teeth into the crisp skin.

"Good *afternoon*, you mean." She laughed, setting the large wooden spoon on a plate on the counter and turning to face him. "The *signora* is out for the day.

Your young lady said she tired of waiting and to give you this."

Maria plunged her plump fingers into the pocket of her tomato spattered apron and fished out a crumpled slip of paper. Alec plucked it away impatiently, knowing exactly what he would see before he even glanced at it. He slammed the fruit on the table and brought the paper to his nose.

"How long ago did she leave?" he demanded shortly.

"Maybe an hour? She said you were sleeping and wouldn't mind if she went ahead. I'm sorry, *Signore* Alec, should have I come to get you sooner?" The elderly woman wrung her hands and looked up at him with a worried frown creasing her brow.

"No, no, it's fine, Maria. I'll, uh, just meet her there." He patted her arm.

"*Va bene.* I'll leave this on the stove for you, and there is fresh bread to go with it." She bustled back to the stove and turned off the flame. Hanging her apron on a hook behind the door, she turned to leave. "*A domani.*"

"Yeah, see you tomorrow," Alec replied absently, as the kitchen door closed behind her. He drew in a deep, cleansing breath, blowing it out through clenched teeth. He glanced at the paper again, shoved it into the pocket of his jeans, and faded to the *Borgo.*

The complex, plaintive strains of Rachmaninoff filled the air as he materialized inside the third floor flat. Her back to him, Tessa's fingers flew over the keys, oblivious to everything except the music. Though some artists shied away from the lush grandeur of this composer's pieces, and the intensity of emotion required to perform them well, Tessa lacked neither courage nor passion. As her long fingers softly struck the final chord and came to rest quietly on the keys, her breath caught on a sob and her body shuddered. The somber Russian's compositions always resonated with Barachiel. Perhaps, the former angel identified with Rachmaninoff's grief over the loss of a way of life, of being a man divorced from his past. Alec swallowed hard over the knot rising to clog his throat and his earlier irritation faded away. He understood now why she'd come alone. Tessa played for her father. She was saying good-bye.

"Rhapsody on a Theme of Paganini in A minor," he said. "His favorite."

Though she hadn't turned around, Tessa knew he was there. The awareness of his presence sizzled along her nerve endings the moment he materialized behind her. "You remembered."

"I remember a lot of things."

"Not all of them bad, I hope?" She turned slowly on the piano stool, eyes narrowed in his direction. She anticipated his anger for setting out on her own, but his casual stance and placid expression gave nothing away. His gaze locked on hers, unblinking, unreadable. As she tugged her gloves from the pocket of her jeans and slipped them on, she wished she could discern even a single one of his thoughts, but his mind remained locked tight from the moment she barreled into his chest at the hospital. Still, the way he looked at her now made her almost believe—Of course, she hadn't gotten much sleep, so it was entirely possible she was hallucinating.

"Most of them incredibly, unforgettably good," he

said at last, breaking the silence and glancing away toward the window. "With one notable exception."

"And we're back to that." Tessa sighed and rose slowly to her feet. "One moment of flawed judgment, one desperate, defensive decision compounded by two massive cases of insecurity, and sprinkled with a hefty helping of wounded pride. I guess it will always come back to that."

Alec's massive shoulders rose and fell. Tessa sighed again and crossed to the pile of cardboard cartons awaiting her attention in the corner. She wrapped her arms around the top box and yanked it against her chest, grunting as she absorbed the unexpected weight. Alec turned from his contemplation of the street below, and crossed the room in two long strides, plucking the container from her arms as though it weighed nothing. He dropped it on the table against the opposite wall that she cleared earlier and stepped away. Tessa dusted her gloved hands down the sides of her jeans and moved around him, tearing at the packing tape and jerking open the flaps.

"Thanks," she muttered.

"Gloves?"

"Not ready to be smacked in the head with the memories just yet."

"Ah." He hesitated. She thought perhaps he might let it drop for the moment, but his next words negated that hope. "I don't know how to overlook it, Tess. Did you expect I would?"

"No." Tessa blew at a stray wisp of hair that escaped the loose knot on top of her head, and lifted a stack of papers from the box, gripping them until her knuckles turned white. "I never expected you to overlook it. I expected you to be furious. I expected you to rant and rave. I expected you to be shocked out of your complacency for five damn minutes, but to ultimately see through it for what it was. I expected..." Her breath caught in her throat. She'd expected—hoped—to discover she was more important to him than his precious research. Instead, he regarded her coldly, like some contemptible specimen that crawled out from under a rock, and then closed his heart and mind to her as firmly as he closed his office door in her face. She took a childish gamble, and she lost. Everything. "I expected you to fight."

"For a woman who preferred someone else?"

"No. For me. Your wife. The other half of your soul. For a woman who not only loved you with every fiber of her being, but was intrinsically incapable of betraying you. You should have known that. Yet, given the most circumstantial evidence, how easily you jumped to conclusions, how easily you believed the worst of me."

"I know what I saw."

"You know what you *think* you saw. I should have explained right then and there, but I was hurt and angry. You know what they say, even negative attention is attention. I've since realized that isn't true, by the way. So, I ran with it. I expected you to fight for me, for us. You didn't. Instead, you snatched away the one tiny sliver of yourself I believed still belonged to me. Then you retreated. You refused to listen."

Hearing his sharply indrawn breath, Tessa spun to face him, finding he'd come to stand uncomfortably close. He gazed down at her from his great height, blue eyes wide, jaw clenched as tightly as the hands fisted at his sides. A nerve jumped in his cheek. Well, he refused to listen back then, but he sure as hell was listening now. Tessa crossed her arms over her chest and lifted her chin.

"And, God help me, I refused to beg. I hope your pride kept you warm at night these last ten years, Alec. I know mine sure as hell hasn't."

"What are you say—" Alec began in a choked voice. He'd let her down on one of the most important nights of her life. He knew that. He also knew he'd been blind to a lot of things back then, but there *was* a man with her that night. He'd seen it with his own eyes. Still, one night, one embrace, didn't necessarily translate to an affair. Unless you were a man painting the picture with a brush dipped in a healthy portion of guilt.

"I'm saying we're both a couple of fools and it's really hard to decide who deserves the grand prize." Her lips compressed into a tight, thin line. Uncrossing her arms, she glanced around at the contents of the apartment and shivered. "I knew my father was a collector, but I think after I moved to the States he crossed the line into hoarder territory. How will I ever get through all of this? I—" The distinctive zing of evil raced up his spine. Tessa's abrupt silence and wide eyes indicated she felt it, too.

"It might just be Gia coming upstairs for something," Alec said slowly, struggling to turn his attention from Tessa's words and concentrate on the potential threat at hand.

"Gia?"

"Giovanna Moscato. She owns this building and the pastry shop downstairs. Both she and her uncle

Enrico, a former *Defensori*, keep apartments here. She's half *Fallen,* so she triggers the alarms when she's close enough."

"Okay." Tessa tore off her gloves and stuffed them back in her pocket. Then she hurried across the room, and began quickly laying her hands on each box in the stack. "But, just in case—"

"What in the hell are you doing?"

Neither of the two sets of footsteps Alec heard plodding down the hall in the direction of the door sounded like a woman. Tessa spun from the corner and pushed past him, sprinting into the bedroom where more stacks of boxes waited. Alec stayed right on her heels as she ran her sensitive fingers over first one carton, then another.

"Tessa. Let's go. I need to get you out of here." Alec gripped her shoulders from behind and attempted to turn her in his arms as a door banged open down the hall, but she shrugged him off and continued her odd behavior. Damn, he should have packed a weapon, but he never expected he'd need one. His mouth went dry and his heart raced as someone stopped outside the door. Thank the saints the door remained locked. He wouldn't hesitate to take on the scum, armed or otherwise, but he had Tessa to consider. He would not put her at risk. "It's definitely not Gia. I'm guessing it's *animorti.* I'm not armed and I need to get you out of here. Now move!"

"Wait. Just give me another second. Where is it?" she mumbled under her breath as her hands flew over one box after another. "Where in the hell did he…here, this one!"

"What the—?" A heavy thud was followed by a

shout. Alec recognized the deep voice and uneven gait of Enrico Moscato as he charged down the hall from his flat. He might be retired from the *Defensori*, and operating on a prosthetic leg, but the man remained as deadly as ever. A couple of *animorti*, low-lifes with a thirst for power duped and inducted by the *Fallen* as expendable servants, were no match for his skill. Tessa tugged ineffectually at a cardboard carton buried under three others.

"For the love of..." Still having no idea what she was doing or why, Alec reached around her and heaved it free, leaving the others to tumble to the floor.

"Yep. That one goes with us. Now, if you've finished standing there looking pretty, McAllister, sounds like we've got company, and I'm really not prepared to entertain."

"Enrico can handle them, but yeah, we should go." Knowing Enrico, Alec suspected the *animorti* were already puddles of black slime, but just in case, he sent out a mental question on the channel used by all *Earthbound* to confirm it. The low rumble of laughter he received in return verified the retired warrior had the situation well in hand and enjoyed the unanticipated exercise.

Keeping the carton securely tucked under one arm, Alec reached out and pulled Tessa to him with the other, though he knew she could have easily faded back to the villa on her own. Her arms came around his waist without hesitation, and she buried her face in his chest. In seconds, they stood in one another's arms in the kitchen of the villa in *Trestevere*.

Chapter Seven

"Well, that was unexpected," Alec observed, feeling Tessa's arms tighten around him briefly. Then she stepped back and tugged the box from under his arm. She set it on the enormous farmhouse table and pushed it away slightly, drawing her hands back as though something might jump out to bite her.

"It's been so long since I ran into one of them, I almost forgot what it felt like."

"What do you mean?" Tessa's super sensitivity had always been an unerring early alert system for evil. *Why would it change?*

Tessa drew in a deep breath and blew it out.

"I told you, I moved to the States."

"What difference does that make?" The U.S. certainly had its fair share of evil ones. "Rome doesn't have the monopoly on the *Fallen* population. In fact, their numbers are usually lower here, since it's Michael's home base."

"I've been teaching at a small, privately funded conservatory in Kentucky for the last couple of years. Underprivileged kids who exhibit extraordinary musical talent. Incredibly rewarding. The area is in the mountains, rather isolated and off the grid. I guess nothing there drew them."

"I see."

"But, you know what's been bothering me? As

much as I loved it, I could have taken a leave of absence and come back at any time. My father knew that. Why didn't he let me know how ill he really was? Why did he wait until there was a very real chance I wouldn't have time to say good-bye? And why, in the name of all that's holy, did he contact *you*?"

Stung by her remark, but damned if he'd show it, Alec shrugged. "Because he knew I'd come, I guess. He said he didn't want you to be alone."

"I understand, but didn't you find it odd, or feel there must be more to it?" She searched his face, as though he might have the answer to a dying old man's idiosyncratic behavior. "He knew he was dying. Why move everything here, check into a hospital, and only contact me at the bitter end?"

"I'll admit, I found the whole situation a bit off. Maybe he wanted to spare you watching the decline. It was difficult enough for me to see him in that state. I can't imagine what it was like for you. He didn't leave much time for questions or lengthy discussions, did he?"

"Exactly. And just for the record, it isn't right, you know. That whole the-Brothers-will-take-care-of-it thing. No body, no funeral, no peaceful grave on the side of a hill, no place to visit. Do you know why I went to the apartment alone today? I hoped I'd find him, some sense of him, something. Surrounded by his things, in the end I discovered they're really only things, aren't they? He wasn't there and it wasn't home. Then again, we always moved around so much, I guess we never had a real one."

A pang of regret stabbed him at the wistful note in her voice. "And then you married me, and I dragged you halfway around the world at the drop of a hat. Or the hint of a clue," Alec added. Stepping closer, he reached out and tucked a stray wisp of hair behind her ear, his fingers brushing along the velvety skin of her high cheekbone. "I never gave you much of a home, either, did I?"

"Maybe home is a choice, not a place." Tessa stepped back, breaking the contact and ignoring the opening he'd provided. Her tongue darted out to lick her lips, and she twisted her fingers together in front of her, a nervous gestures so familiar to him. "So, as I started to say back at the flat, my father was quite a collector. Art, music, manuscripts…he loved beautiful things. I guess, given his origins, it's not so surprising. It's going to take me weeks to go through and catalog it all. I'll end up donating most of it to libraries and museums, I suppose."

"I promised I'd help you, and I will." It was the least he could do for the man who'd been his friend and mentor, right? And, yeah, for Tessa, too. "You don't have to do this alone, you know."

"I know, and I appreciate it." Tessa cleared her throat and reached out to slide the carton toward him. "Until I can get to the rest of it, this box is for you."

"What is it?"

Tessa shook her head and nudged the box in his direction. "I don't know. He only told me he'd planted a memory on the box itself so I could detect it by touch. Something he was working on and didn't have time to finish? Said you'd figure it out and know what to do."

"No hint as to what it is?"

"No, but considering he involved Michael in all this, maybe he found something related to your work?"

"He knew I worked for Michael?" Alec reached for the box, slid it closer, and picked at the layers of packing tape sealing the top flaps. His pulse quickened as it always did at the prospect of a new challenge.

"Duh. Of course, he knew, Alec," Tessa sighed, pulling out a chair and sinking into it. Then she reached out to work at the tape on the other side. "When I arrived on his doorstep ten years ago, I wasn't feeling especially charitable toward you or your secrets."

"You went to Barachiel? But, I thought—" He'd thought she'd run to her lover. But, in the last twenty-four hours, he'd begun to re-evaluate not only *that* thought, but a whole lot of others.

"I know what you thought. Being a fool, I encouraged you to think it. I told myself once you calmed down and thought it through, you'd come find me, we'd talk it out, and maybe even laugh about it one day. Never happened. For two relatively smart people with an impressive number of advanced academic degrees, at the end of the day, we both suffer from Book-Smart-Common-Sense-Stupid Syndrome."

"Common sense probably isn't as common as most people think. I'll agree I wasn't exactly open to conversation at the time," Alec said, yanking the tape free, flipping open the box, and peering inside. "I'm listening now."

"Maybe with the ten percent of your brain not currently fixated on what lies hidden at the bottom of that box."

Hands tangled in layers of bubble wrap, Alec glanced up as the chair legs screeched against the tile floor. Tessa rose slowly to her feet and pinned him with an over-bright gaze. His hands stilled, and he withdrew them from the box, swiping his damp palms down the front of his shirt.

"Haven't you ever heard of multi-tasking?" He ignored the part of him longing to rip the box open, and remained focused on his wife.

"You know what I think?" Tessa raised a brow. "I think my father waited until the bitter end intending to extract deathbed promises from each of us, knowing neither of us could refuse."

"Why would he do that?"

"Because he loved us." A sad, fleeting smile briefly crossed her face. "He hated that we were apart, but he never took sides. Of course, it doesn't mean he didn't also believe we were two idiots nursing our grievances and hiding behind our wounded pride. Maybe he thought forcing us together would prompt a conversation he believed we should have had a long time ago."

Alec sucked in a long breath. Didn't Michael say almost the same thing? Ten years, a tiny blip in the long life of an *Earthbound*, but maybe time enough to put aside recriminations and actually communicate?

"You mean like two mature, reasonable adults instead of two offended, angry children?"

Her lips quirked. "Something like that."

"Assuming we were going to have this conversation, how do you think it would go?" Alec asked slowly, pushing the box away, removing temptation from his reach.

Tessa watched him shove the box aside, then gazed up at him with a hopeful expression, and something shifted in his heart.

"Hypothetically." Alec crossed his arms over his

chest and swallowed hard.

"Well, hypothetically, I'd start by reminding you how you were consumed by work. Every day you buried yourself in your research, and every day I died a little inside as you descended deeper into your world and spent less and less time in mine. I tried to be philosophical about it. I mean, we live for centuries, right? The obsession was bound to wane eventually, and I'd have you back. I'm not making excuses for my actions, just trying to help you understand the motivation behind them."

"Fair enough. But, hypothetically, weren't you equally consumed?" Alec countered. "It's not like you were sitting around twiddling your thumbs. You composed an entire symphony during that time, for God's sake."

"What did you expect me to do? Sit around and do nothing? I had to do something while I waited you out." Tessa lifted a shoulder and lowered her eyes.

"It was more than a little something to kill time. It was damned brilliant, Tessa. The London Philharmonic doesn't perform just anything."

"No, they don't, do they?" She blinked up at him with a faint smile. "It was...overwhelming. And nerve wracking. Every music critic on the continent was there to weigh in with an opinion."

"And you dazzled them all, just as I knew you would." He always recognized her singular gift, her incredible talent. He always had faith in her ability, even when she doubted it herself.

"Yes, I did. The critics, the audience, our families, pretty much everyone that mattered." Her lips compressed into a tight, thin line and her hands curled into fists. "Everyone, that is, except the person I composed it *for*. The person who mattered most. Even when I realized you weren't coming, I swallowed the tears and waited some more. But, you couldn't tear yourself away, not for five minutes, not even on one of the most important nights of my life. How do you think it looked, Alec? How do you think it *felt*?"

"I lost track of time," Alec muttered, suddenly unable to meet her eyes, and realizing how lame his excuse sounded. Running late, he promised to meet her at the Royal Festival Hall, so Tessa went on ahead with her father and the others. He showered and donned his tux, then stopped in his office, intending only to better organize the stack of letters to make them easier to sort through later. But, then he stopped to read one. And then he resolved to read just one more, and before he realized it, he'd scanned over half the pile and looked up at the clock with a stone settling in his gut. He missed the entire performance. "I know it's no excuse. I screwed up. But, you couldn't really have believed anyone or anything was more important to me than—"

"Couldn't I? Be honest with yourself and look at it from my perspective, Alec. What would you think in my shoes? Did you ever find it?"

"What?"

"The Ring of Aandalena. Did you find it?"

"No. I mean, yes it's been found. But, no, none of my research led to the recovery. Long story." And a waste of time that drove a wedge between them.

"I see. So, I guess there's no point in asking whether it was worth it. We both know the answer. Hypothetically. Of course, hindsight is always twenty-twenty, isn't it? After the concert ended, I made excuses for your absence, plastered on a smile, and danced my way through one party after another. I put on a hell of a performance, determined to see it through to the bitter end, with or without you. Finally, the last glass of champagne was consumed, the music fell silent, and there was nothing left to do except come home."

"You had every right to be hurt and angry. I was fully prepared to grovel."

"Funny, you didn't appear to be groveling at all. You appeared to be a selfish jerk who accused rather than apologized."

"I waited. But, when the hours passed, and you didn't answer your phone, didn't come home, I realized you were right. I *had* shut you out, though not deliberately. I *did* take you for granted. It felt like a blinding, painful light snapped on in a dark room and illuminated every word you'd been trying to pound into my thick skull for months. I finally got it. I planned to tell you and find a way to make it up to you. And then I heard a car, looked out the window, and saw you in another man's arms—" His voice cracked, as the picture replayed in his memory like a bad movie on a continuous loop. "It broke me, Tessa, and I've never figured out how to put the pieces back together. The thought of you in someone else's bed, the knowledge I'd pushed you there. Something snapped. I couldn't think straight. I hoped—prayed—I was wrong. But, then you sauntered in all smeared and disheveled, and you didn't deny it. How do you think *that* felt?"

"You witnessed comfort that night, not passion. Someone who showed up, who was *there* for me when I needed him. You want to talk about my *alleged* infidelity? Let's discuss *yours*, shall we?"

"*Mine*? I was never unfaithful to you."

"Weren't you? Your work was an ever changing, always fascinating, all consuming mistress with whom I couldn't compete." She drew in a shaky breath and blew it out again. "Well, that night I had your undivided attention at last, didn't I? Yes, I chose the wrong weapon to obtain it—a stupid, spiteful weapon—one I knew would hurt you. But, when you jumped to conclusions and made it *so* easy...I ran with it. I couldn't seem to stop, even when I saw the pain on your face. God forgive me, Alec, I *wanted* to hurt you. Because you hurt me, too."

"Comfort, passion...call it what you like. In my book, sex is sex, Tess."

"Well, maybe you should take a closer look at that book of yours. Stop reading between the lines and concentrate on the black and white right in front of your eyes. Are you being deliberately obtuse or are you really incapable of seeing the truth?"

"You were my wife, dammit!"

"I'm still your wife, you jackass. I always have been. And you still can't see anything beyond the end of your nose. This conversation is over." She turned on her heel and moved in the direction of the door. Alec's hand shot out and grabbed her arm, spinning her back toward him and hauling her hard against him. She struggled to free herself, and his arms locked around her like steels bands, pinning the length of her body against his.

"It's over when *I* say it's over."

Alec crushed his mouth to hers with a growl, bending her back over his arm, and plunged his tongue between her lips like a weapon. He ground his hips into her, making clear the effect she still had on him. She tasted of honey, and mint, and everything he'd been missing in his life for ten long years. For better or for worse, together or apart, she was *his*. And it was damn well time she realized it. He felt the moment she softened. With a pained whimper, she gripped the front of his shirt, pressed her breasts against him, and wrapped her tongue around his. He tore his mouth away, breathing heavily.

"Did he make you feel the way I do, Tessa? Did his kisses melt your bones?" Alec buried his face in the side of her neck and nipped his way from her collarbone to her ear, brushing back the heavy fall of her hair to trace the shell-like curve with the tip of his tongue. He tightened his arms around her as a shudder ran through her. Her pulse raced against his lips like the frantic heart of a captive bird. He'd intended to tease the hell out of her, torture her, remind her of what she so easily abandoned, and then walk away and leave her wanting. Judging by his own churning gut, rock hard erection, and aching balls, his plan backfired miserably.

Damn, he still wanted her. She'd run to her father, moved to the States. Alone. Not with a lover. Maybe it was nothing more than a one night stand. That's what she'd been trying to tell him. If she'd been unfaithful, it wasn't habitual, and he knew at least part of the culpability belonged to him. Yes, he still wanted her. Wanted her like air to breathe, with a heart-stopping desperation he forgot he could feel, something he never felt with anyone else in all the long centuries of his life. Forgive her? His heart already had. But, the inability of his pride to forget kept his gut twisted in knots.

"Did his lips taste every sweet, honey-flavored inch of you? Did he make you crave the feel of him buried so deep inside your body you couldn't tell where you left off and he began? Is that what he did?"

"No," she choked. "No one ever—"

"Will complete you the way I do?" He finished for her, lifting his head and tracing a finger along the smooth line of her jaw. Then he rubbed his thumb along her full lower lip. "Bound mates, two halves of the same soul. My only consolation these last ten years has been the certainty that no matter who shared your bed, deep inside you suffered the same emptiness I did."

With his gaze locked to hers, Alec pried her fingers free from his shirt. Bringing her hand to his lips, he turned it over, and pressed a warm, moist kiss into her palm. She curled her fingers into a fist and pressed it to her chest as though she could hold it there. A warm spark of desire burned in her eyes and sent a heated flush into her cheeks. God, how he'd missed her. Without her, he'd only been half alive.

Alec buried his fingers in her hair and cupped her face, tilting it up to his. Tessa offered no resistance, leaning into him and sliding her hands up the hard planes of his chest to wrap around his neck, tangling her fingers in the curls at his nape.

"Mine." The thought escaped of its own accord, slipping through the locked barriers he'd erected around his thoughts since she slammed into his chest in the hospital corridor.

"Mine." Her voice echoed in his head.

With a low groan, he captured her lips again, pressing her against him with a hand splayed across her buttocks, while using the other to sweep everything, including the open box, from the top of the table. He stretched her back against the unforgiving wood and lowered his body over hers. Many things changed in the past ten years, he thought. But, some things never would.

Chapter Eight

"While I'm thrilled to see the two of you getting along so well, at last count there were four bedrooms in this villa. You couldn't control the wild monkey sex long enough to spare my kitchen table? Oh, well, I suppose that's why God invented bleach."

"My mother, the queen of impeccable timing," Alec grumbled against Tessa's lips. Shielded from Madge's sight by his body, Tessa fumbled beneath him, forcing her hands between them and frantically yanking the edges of her blouse together while scrabbling to fasten the buttons. Alec glanced down, confirmed she'd managed to cover herself, and levered away from her, and straightened, tugging his T-shirt down. Then he reached for her hand and pulled her up beside him.

"What do you know about wild monkey sex? Never mind, you're my mother. I don't want to know. I thought you had dinner plans."

"Probably a wise decision on your part. But, just for the record, I'm mature, not dead. And change of plans. Clearly." Madge's lips twitched as she crossed her arms over her chest and stared pointedly at Tessa's. Alec followed her gaze and smirked as the heat crawled up Tessa's neck and blazed into her cheeks. She hadn't even come close to doing up the buttons correctly, and her blouse gaped open in some areas and hung at a cock-eyed angle in others.

"Might I suggest pullovers, dear? So much more convenient in a pinch."

"Duly noted," Tessa muttered under her breath, tugging ineffectually at the hem, and then showing them both her back to undo the buttons and repair the damage.

"I thought you were going to the flat this afternoon," Madge observed as Tessa turned back to face them, decently covered at last. "Knowing your father and his love of beautiful things, I imagine there's quite a lot to sort through."

"We did and there is, but we didn't get much accomplished," Alec replied, stepping forward to help his mother who'd bent to retrieve the items he'd pushed to the floor. He shoved the trailing bubble wrap into the box and plunked it on the table. "We were interrupted."

Madge chuckled. "So you have a theme going?"

"By *animorti*," Tessa interjected quickly. "We left in a bit of a hurry."

"*Animorti*?" A frown pleated Madge's smooth forehead. "What on Earth were they doing there?"

"No idea, but at least they provided Enrico with a little entertainment. Turns out the flat Barachiel rented is in Gia's building."

"Enrico? How is the dear man? I really must stop by and see him one of these days. It's been far too long."

"We didn't stick around to chat, Mother," Alec returned dryly. "I wasn't armed and my priority was Tessa's safety. Enrico had things well in hand."

"No doubt. He does love a good fight. So, what's this?" She gestured to the box.

"Don't know. We were just about to find out,"

Alec tugged at the plastic while Madge straightened the quilted placemats on the table.

"Oh, is *that* what you were doing?"

"Yes, that's exactly what we were doing." Face flaming, a self-conscious grin tugged at the corner of Tessa's lips. They *had* been just about to find out, but for the first time in ages, Alec's attention focused on his wife instead of his insatiable curiosity. Something like that could give a girl hope. At least he made it clear he still wanted her, even if he hadn't yet found a way to forgive her. It was a start. Tessa stepped forward and batted Alec's hands away, plunging her own into the box to retrieve whatever lay hidden in the layers of protective wrapping. "Let's see what we've got, shall we?"

Preoccupied by Alec's expression as he watched her, she curled her fingers around the rectangular object at the bottom of the box and drew it free. A tsunami of memories crashed into her, buckling her knees and stealing her breath. Acting quickly, Madge wrenched the item from her unresisting fingers.

"Tess..." Alec's face paled as he caught her limp body around the waist and dragged her against him before she hit the hard ceramic floor.

"I'm okay," she breathed, gripping his shirt tightly and leaning against him for support. "I'm okay. So stupid...I wasn't thinking. It doesn't happen every time."

"Hence the reason it's called a gift and not a superpower," Madge offered, placing the ornately decorated wooden casket on the table.

"My mother's wedding box," Tessa whispered from the safe confines of Alec's arms.

"I remember it," Madge smiled. Made entirely of wood, but appearing to be cast in gold, the heavily gilded container was nearly eighteen inches long and a foot wide, standing nine inches tall at the highest point of the domed lid. "Your father acquired it from a dealer in Ferrara over two centuries ago. The decorations are modeled in *pastiglia*, a technique popular in northern Italy during the Renaissance. This piece was done with a white lead paste mixed with egg white and perfumed with musk. The scent was thought to have aphrodisiacal properties. He gave it to your mother as a wedding gift."

Shaking her head slightly, Tessa straightened away from Alec to stand on her own. He let her move away, but then slid his hand up her back, under the fall of her hair, to cup her nape, his long fingers soothing the tense muscles knotted at the base of her skull. Her knees threatened to give way again, but this time it had nothing to do with rogue memories of her mother. Who needed a gilded box perfumed with musk to act as an aphrodisiac with him around? With his other hand, Alec reached around her to twist the brass catch and flip open the domed lid, revealing an empty, relatively shallow cavity lined in wine colored velvet.

"My mother used to tell me the story when I was little. I was so young when she died, it's one of the few true memories I have of her without the use of my so-called gift."

"Whatever your father's intent in setting this aside for me, it clearly means a great deal to you, Tess. I want you to keep it."

Tessa drew in a long slow breath and released it, carefully settling her shields in place. She smiled inwardly when Alec pulled her back as she reached for the casket again.

"It's okay. I'm prepared this time. And thank you, Alec. This does mean a great deal to me, but I'm pretty sure the casket itself isn't what my father wanted you to have."

"What do you mean?"

"I mean..." Tessa felt carefully around the inside edges until she found what she was looking for. Pressing a finger to the spot where the sides met the bottom, she slid the unobtrusive lever to the left, and with a faint click, the bottom rose up on one side. "False bottom. It's so well done that if you weren't aware of it, you'd never find it."

"But, you knew about it."

"Yes, my mother showed it to me." Tessa lifted the panel and withdrew a packet wrapped in thick oilskin and tied securely with string. Handing it over her shoulder to Alec, she felt around to ensure she didn't miss anything, and pressed the velvet covered wood back into place. Then she carefully lowered the lid into place and refastened the catch.

"Well, as much as I'd love to see what's in there, you can fill me in later. I have work to do." Madge flapped her hands at them. "Luca called earlier and he and Callista will be arriving soon, so while I finish cleaning up this mess, maybe you could take your new toys into the den?"

"She's awfully close to term. Should she be traveling?" Alec asked.

"Probably not, but you know your sister. Luca tried to talk her out of it, but she's determined to have me with her when she delivers. I told her I'd come to New

York, but she's decided she wants the baby to be born in Italy in deference to Luca's heritage."

"Callista? I don't understand." Tessa said, looking from one to the other. The only Callista she knew was Alec's younger sister, and she'd been murdered by a *Fallen* named Jacques Rapier, known to the mortal world as Jack the Ripper, over a century ago.

"I guess with everything else going on, Alec neglected to tell you," Madge glared at Alec and smiled at Tessa. "Callista is alive and well! After all those years believing her dead, I sometimes still have to pinch myself." Madge glowed. "She and Luca are expecting their first child nearly any day. Can you believe it? I'm going to be a grandmother."

"She's *alive*?" Tessa forcibly snapped her gaping jaw closed and turned instinctively to embrace Alec as tears pricked the back of her lids. The loss of his sister had been a quiet shadow looming over him for as long as she'd known him. She couldn't even imagine what it must feel like to have found her. After a moment's hesitation, his arms came around her and hugged her in return. Tipping her head back, she rested her chin on his chest and looked directly in his eyes. "I am happier for you than words can express. Truly."

Alec's throat worked, and he blinked rapidly, then he squeezed her again. "Thank you. It's pretty amazing to have her back."

Tessa stepped out of Alec's arms, and turned to embrace her mother-in-law.

"I've no doubt you'll be a marvelous grandmother, but, I have to say, I doubt you'll ever look like one."

"One does what one can with what one has," Madge patted her dark hair and winked. Though not immortal, *Earthbound* aged so slowly after the age of thirty-five, that though centuries old, Magdalena McAllister remained a handsome woman who could pass for someone in her late-forties. "Now, both of you, out of my kitchen so I can straighten up. Oh, and Tessa? I'm afraid I put you in Callista's room last night. I hope you don't mind if I have your things moved to the other bedroom down the hall."

"Would that be the one connected to mine? Subtle, Mother." Alec frowned.

"You know it's the only available room, Alec." She pressed a hand to her chest and blinked innocently. "Why must you assume everything is a conspiracy?"

"Because when you're involved, it generally is." Alec's lips curled. "You're not the only one who wasn't born yesterday."

"Listen, I can stay at the flat."

"No," Alec and his mother exclaimed simultaneously.

"Didn't you say there were *animorti* there this afternoon?" Madge rushed on quickly. "We have no idea who or what they may have been looking for. You will stay right here where you're safe, young lady."

"Alec could set *sigils* around the place. That should keep the riff-raff out," Tessa said, referring to the ancient symbols used as a form of protection by *Earthbound* to keep out anyone except those whose molecular signatures were woven into the angelic characters. "And there's a former *Defensori* living right down the hall."

"Yes, I could, but my mother would still worry. In fact, I doubt she'd sleep a wink." He cleared his throat. "If you won't think of yourself, at least consider her feelings."

"Well, of course I don't want your mother to worry. I didn't want to inconvenience anyone."

"That's settled then," Madge announced, waving her hands in the direction of the parlor. "Now, shoo, both of you. I have a table to bleach."

Chapter Nine

Alec ushered Tessa into the study, closed the door, and then moved around behind the desk, keeping his gaze pointedly averted from hers.

"Alec, don't you think we should talk about—"

"Not now, Tess. Just…not now. I'm sorry. I don't know what I was thinking. My anger got the better of me and—" If his mother hadn't interrupted, he knew he would have taken Tessa right there on the kitchen table like some mindless animal.

"Don't." Tessa whispered in a strangled voice. "I'd much rather ignore the big purple elephant in the room than know anger is all that's left between us."

He grimaced. "I think we've just proven otherwise."

"But, desire isn't forgiveness, is that what you're trying to say?"

"I have no freaking idea what I'm trying to say." He shouted, slamming the packet on top of the desk with enough force to send papers flying in the air. He sucked in a deep breath and scrubbed a hand over his face. Then he met Tessa's pained gaze and continued in a quieter voice. "I'm tied in knots here, Tess. So until I figure it out, I think it's better not to talk about it. Okay?"

She regarded him steadily for a moment, swallowed hard, and dropped her gaze to her hands. For the first time. Alec noticed she still wore her wedding band. Twisting it around and around on her finger, she finally nodded.

"Aren't you going to open it?"

"What?"

"The packet. Don't you want to see what's inside?"

"Oh." He'd completely forgotten about it. "Yeah, I guess."

Alec undid the string while Tessa looked on from the other side of the desk. He peeled back the oilskin covering to reveal a packet of papers folded in thirds to letter size. He separated them and spread them over the top of the desk. Most appeared to be copies of telegrams and aerial maps, many stamped Top Secret, with later notations they'd been declassified. Mixed in with these official looking documents were a few newspaper clippings, a pocket sized spiral notebook, and a poorly done sketch of an ornate necklace drawn in a childish hand.

"Give me that," Tessa snatched the drawing from under his fingers. "How on Earth did this get in here?"

"What is it?"

"Can't you tell? It's a priceless work of art, of course." Tessa bit her lip and glanced up at Alec through her lashes. "A masterpiece I drew when I was a child."

"Um. Tess? Don't quit your day job."

"Very funny. I can't believe my father kept this all these years. And what's it doing with these things he left for you?"

"Maybe he thought it had a connection to something?"

"I can't imagine what." Tessa shrugged.

"Why don't you tell me about it. Maybe we can figure it out together."

"You never ask for my input when it involves your work."

Alec cleared his throat. "I'm asking now."

"And people claim miracles don't exist. Okay, let's see…it was toward the end of the Second World War." Tessa drew her brows together and crinkled her forehead. "I guess I was about ten or so."

"The second World War and you were ten." Alec shook his head and picked up the photographs. "Sometimes, I forget how young you really are."

"Only because you're over the hill."

"*Touché*." He looked up and smiled, then frowned as he returned his attention to the desk top, rearranging the photos. A lock of dark hair tumbled over his forehead as he leaned in for a closer look. Knowing it would feel as thick and silky as she remembered, Tessa's fingers itched to reach out and brush it back. Instead, she curled them into a fist until her nails bit into her palm.

"I know that look, Alec McAllister. What are you thinking?"

"I'm not sure yet." His gaze darted back and forth between the photos and the drawing, then widened. "These maps represent cities all over Italy. See these white blocks? They appear to correspond with historical sites and monuments."

"Is that significant?"

"Could be. The Nazis were notorious plunderers of art, cultural property, and any other treasures they could get their hands on. They engaged in a massive campaign to steal valuables—artwork, jewelry, gold—

from their enemies and even former allies, like Italy."

"Not to mention their campaign to systematically exterminate entire peoples," Tessa interrupted, her voice laced with undisguised disgust.

"Sadly, true. Not surprisingly, a good number of *Fallen* existed among the upper echelon of the Third Reich. But, just as many *Earthbound* were scattered across the globe working against them." He picked up one of the missives and quickly scanned it. "Interesting."

"What?"

"This is a copy of a secret communication from Dwight D. Eisenhower to the commanders of the various military branches in the European Theater of Operations emphasizing the importance of preserving historical monuments." He tossed it on the desk and picked up another. "This one is an urgent, top secret telegram from General Marshall to General Eisenhower about a quantity of gold, foreign currency, and art treasures captured by the American forces in Germany. He was asking permission to move it to a place of safekeeping in the American occupied zone of Germany and keep it carefully guarded pending study and consultation with the Allies."

Tessa snatched up a page, squinting to decipher the faded text. Then she opened her eyes wide.

"Oh, my God! This one says they found two hundred and fifty tons of gold bullion and over two thousand boxes of fine art buried in a German salt mine. Two hundred and fifty tons of gold? Where did it all come from?"

Alec frowned. "Some stolen from banks on the Nazi march across the continent, no doubt. Some of it…well, you probably don't want to know."

"No, I probably don't." Her heart ached for the lives lost and families torn apart. Innocent people robbed of freedom and dignity, stripped of their humanity, possessions, and even the gold fillings from their teeth to finance a madman's heinous agenda.

"I suspect these documents are related to the Monuments, Fine Arts, and Archives program, or MFAA. It looks like your father worked with the Venus Fixers. I'll be damned." He looked up, his face creased in a grin.

"Venus Fixers?"

"Most people knew them better as Monuments Men. They were a small volunteer corps of historians, architects, museum curators, and professors put together by the Allies. They worked both on the front lines and behind them to mitigate combat damage to significant art and monuments, as well as track and recover stolen art treasures. Many of them went on to have prolific careers in the foremost cultural institutions in the world after the war. In Italy, the troops gave them the nickname the Venus Fixers, because they not only protected and recovered great artistic treasures, but when damage was unavoidable, they also worked to restore it."

"Oh, that. I didn't know the project had an official title." Tessa shrugged. "Yes, my father worked closely with the director of the *Galleria della Uffizi* and others, organizing the evacuation of art from Florence to privately owned *villas* and *palazzos* in the countryside. If a treasure couldn't be relocated, they did their best to protect it on site. Churches were sandbagged, windows boarded, the doors of the *Battistero di San Giovanni* were removed and hidden away. Artisans built what amounted to brick tombs around Michelangelo's David and other priceless statues. Of course, everyone felt this to be precautionary. No one really believed the fighting would ever progress so far north."

"I didn't know he'd been involved, though it doesn't surprise me. Barachiel and I lost touch for a number of years during the war. I spent my time in Britain working with the cryptanalysts at the Government Code and Cypher School in Bletchley Park. Your father remained in Italy. And afterwards…well, no one was especially anxious to talk about the things they'd seen or done."

"I imagine you found the city much different from what you remembered by the time you came to Florence to visit my father. Though at least they'd rebuilt the bridges by then." For weeks they heard rumors the Nazis were planning to blow up all of the city bridges spanning the Arno. The Nazi commander in Italy believed destruction of the bridges would slow down the Allies' advance and assure the German army's safe retreat to the north. She would never forget that hot, August night. When the first explosion came, Tessa thought the world was ending. She clung to her father, both of them with tears in their eyes, as the blasts continued throughout the night. By morning all that remained over the river was the *Ponte Vecchio* and a thick cloud of dark smoke.

"Many things changed. Especially you. You certainly weren't the little girl I remembered."

Alec lifted his gaze from his contemplation of the papers and captured hers across the desk. Tessa's breath caught in her throat. She remembered that day as clearly as if it had been yesterday instead of more than half a century ago. She thought him the most beautiful man she'd ever seen. A living, breathing work of art. When he opened his mouth to speak, she couldn't hear the words at first, because she heard only music. A symphony plucking at her heart strings. In the first moment, she knew. He was meant to be hers for all time. Or at least until she let her insecurities get the better of her and screwed it up.

"No, I wasn't," she whispered. He held her gaze for a few seconds more, then cleared his throat and looked back down at the desk, and the spell was broken. Once upon a time they moved freely into and out of one another's heads, their thoughts and emotions effortlessly intermingled. Now, his mind was a dark, blank slate she couldn't read, and she kept hers as closely guarded. Swallowing audibly, she stepped around the desk and plastered herself to his side to view the maps from his perspective.

"What makes you think these things are related to this MFAA?" She picked up the drawing. "What could this possibly have to do with it?"

"The missives point to it, and I think these must be reconnaissance maps, marking areas Allied pilots were instructed to avoid on bombing missions."

Alec pushed everything aside and tapped the childish drawing.

"Okay, tell me about this. I doubt your father would have included it unless it had some significance."

Tessa blew out a long breath and nodded.

"Everyone in the area of town surrounding the Arno and the bridges had been evacuated. We took shelter in the *Palazzo Pitti* with hundreds, maybe thousands, of others after the German military occupied the city. The palace's rooms were filled with cooking odors, unwashed bodies, and the constant noise and commotion of displaced people and pets. Quite a different atmosphere than those rooms were used to, I'm sure." Tessa smiled. "My father left early that day, just after the sun came up. About midmorning, a woman came around asking for him. The lady he hired to care for me, well, maybe it's more accurate to say the girl, since she couldn't have been more than eighteen, sent her away. Later, I went outside to get some air and the same woman approached me. She pulled a small, cloth bag from her pocket and pressed it into my hand telling me it was very important I give it to my father, and tell no one else about it."

"The necklace?"

Tessa nodded. "But, of course I didn't know it at the time. I hurried up to the room we slept in, thinking to hide the pouch under my mattress until my father returned. As I pulled it from my sleeve, the necklace fell out. It was beautiful, and without thinking, I picked it up so no one would see. As soon as I touched it... well, let's just say it wasn't beautiful anymore." Tessa handed the drawing to Alec and a shudder moved through her. "The next thing I knew, I'd been taken to a field hospital of some kind. Apparently, I became hysterical and Angelina couldn't locate my father. She told them she didn't know what else to do. Finally, he arrived and took me away."

"And then you told him about the woman and gave him the necklace?"

"I told him about the woman, of course. But, the

necklace was nowhere to be found. And neither was Angelina. We could only assume she'd stolen it and run away. It had to be quite valuable and everyone was suffering, never knowing what the next day would bring. It was a time of fear, desperation, and disbelief. Who could blame her? And so, my father asked me to draw what I remembered."

"And when he saw it, what did he say?"

"I don't remember him saying anything." Tessa looked up at Alec and shook her head. "I drew the picture and gave it to him. He tucked it away and we never spoke of it again. I tried to block all of it from my mind. I can't imagine why he kept it all these years, or why it's mixed together with these papers."

"What are these squiggles on the stone supposed to be?" Alec narrowed his eyes in the direction of the drawing.

"I told you it wasn't a very good likeness," Tessa laughed. "The squiggles, as you call them, are a child's rendition of filigree which surrounded the stone almost completely."

"Maybe it's a *Djinn* trap," interjected a dry, male voice from the doorway.

Tessa's head snapped up at the familiar, cynical tone.

"Well, that can't be good. You just get in? How's Calli?" Alec tossed the drawing on the desk, moved away from Tessa, and strode across the room. Tessa followed slowly, hanging back as the two men pounded one another on the back.

"Yes, we made it and your stubborn sister is fine. Exhausted, but fine."

Finally, Luca Fiorelli turned to face her. Features

perfect and timeless, body long and lean, the Ice Warrior of the *Defensori* remained as impossibly handsome as Tessa remembered. His faded jeans fit as perfectly as if they'd been tailored for him, and a black T-shirt stretched across the broad expanse of his wide shoulders. Not a single strand of the silver blond hair waving back from his high, smooth forehead dared stray out of place. He wore his characteristically unreadable expression, but she noticed his usually cool gray eyes held a warmth and sparkle previously lacking. Quirking a brow, he reached to take both of her hands in his, and leaned forward, greeting her with a kiss on either cheek.

"Hello, Tessa. It's been a long time. My condolences on the loss of your father. A good man."

"Thank you. I don't think his passing has sunk in yet." She swallowed hard, pressing a hand to the hollow spot in her stomach that ached every time she remembered, and forced a smile. "I understand congratulations are in order. I must admit, it surprised me to discover you married with a child on the way."

"No one could be more surprised than I." Luca's normally bland expression lit with a grin. "I find it suits me. My Calli is a gift. A sometimes loud and opinionated gift," he added with a wink as the sound of raised women's voices reached them from the direction of the kitchen. "But, I think I'll keep her."

"I realize she probably had a long and uncomfortable flight, but she just got here. How could she possibly have something to whine about already?" Alec muttered.

"She's not whining, she's ranting. Please note the difference. Apparently, she's a little put out no one bothered to mention you had a wife."

"Oh." Alec glanced at Tessa, and she dropped her gaze to the floor, twisting her fingers together. "Listen, Tess—"

"No, I understand," she whispered.

"It wasn't deliberate. We'd just gotten Calli back, she already had so much to absorb, and things were pretty chaotic. I guess it just never came up—"

"Honestly, I do understand, Alec. I left and you didn't see or hear from me in ten years." Of course, there were months of opportunity to tell his sister after the initial chaos of her return, at the very least. Clearly, he didn't considered their marriage important enough to mention. She glanced up, widened her eyes, and shrugged. "Why on Earth would it come up?" She shifted her gaze back to Luca. "So, what's a *Djinn* trap?"

Chapter Ten

"Exactly what it sounds like. A *Djinn* trap is an object of iron designed to trap and bind *Djinn*."

Luca stepped around Tessa and Alec and moved toward the desk. Picking up the items scattered on its surface one at a time, he gave each careful consideration before moving on to the next.

"But, the necklace didn't look like iron, it looked like gold," Tessa said. "Although, now I think of it, it did feel heavier than it should."

"Seriously, Luca, how could you not know that from the superb drawing?" Alec snorted, crossing his arms over his chest.

"Looks can be deceiving," Luca countered with a fleeting smile. "As for the drawing, I imagine the art world heaved a collective sigh of relief when you chose a musical vocation."

"Though I'm hard pressed to decide which of you is the more talented comedian, you can both keep your clever comments to yourself. I'm well aware I can barely sketch a recognizable stick figure. What's a *Djinn*?"

"Your father never spoke of them?" Tessa shook her head. "Not surprising, I guess. The *Djinn* are little known in the West beyond tales of magic lamps and beautiful women who dissolve into pink smoke and emerge from fancy bottles."

"Genies?" Tessa raised her brows and looked from one man to the other, biting back a laugh. "Really, Luca. How gullible do you think I am? They're a myth, an Arabian fairy tale at best."

"Many would say the same of angels, but we know better, do we not?" Luca grinned at her over the top of her drawing. "*Djinn* are very real. A race created from smokeless fire before the time of Adam. With no defined physical form of their own, they're usually invisible to the naked eye. However, they're also powerful shape-shifters who can take on the physical form of just about anything that suits them."

"Okay," she drawled, glancing at Alec to see if Luca was trying to put one over on her. But, his dark brows were drawn together, and he regarded Luca through narrowed eyes. He didn't look the least bit amused. "So, assuming I'm buying this, are they good or evil?"

"It depends. Created with free will, they choose which path they wish to follow. Though most are not especially enamored with humans. Many believe even supposedly good *Djinn* have their own agenda and should never be trusted completely," Luca answered, tossing everything back on the desk. "Brace yourself, Alec."

"Why should he—" Tess began, but the answer to her half spoken question arrived in the form of a very flushed, very pregnant woman with a murderous gleam in her eye. Callista McAllister Fiorelli stormed into the room and headed directly for Alec. Flinging a long, thick braid of dark hair over her shoulder, she tilted her head back, planted her fists on her hips, and glared at her much larger brother.

"You are an inconsiderate, self-involved snake."

"You are as big as a house."

Luca crossed his arms over his massive chest and shook his head, allowing it to drop back on his shoulders as his wife promptly burst into tears. Chuckling, Alec drew Callista into his arms and dropped a kiss on the top of her head. Then he gripped her shoulders and turned her in his arms to face the others in the room.

"And you have never looked more beautiful. Now stop blubbering and turn around and meet my…wife."

"Hello," Callista sniffed, sagging against her brother. "I'm afraid I've given you a very poor first impression."

"Not at all," Tessa smiled and moved forward to take the other woman's extended hand. "You've had a long flight, you're nearly ready to deliver, and you must be exhausted. Besides, Alec really can be an inconsiderate, self-involved snake, but I'm hopeful he's redeemable."

"I'll believe that when I see it." Calli grinned and jabbed an elbow into Alec's midsection.

"At any rate, I've been away for a long time, and it's understandable my name didn't come up. Please forgive Alec. I'm sure his thoughtlessness was quite unintentional."

"I wonder if that's possible," Alec said quietly, and Tessa's startled gaze flew to his face. Observing his wary expression, compressed lips, and tightly clenched jaw, Tessa had the uneasy feeling the forgiveness he sought was neither his sister's, nor solely related to his failure to mention their marriage. Was he offering her an olive branch? He had no way of knowing with the clarity of time and distance, she'd forgiven him and acknowledged her own contribution to their estrangement years ago. What kept her silent and withdrawn all those years had been the fear of his rejection and inability to believe or forgive *her*. In danger of becoming lost in the depths of his eyes, and keenly aware of their all too interested audience, Tessa bit her lip and looked away.

"Well, you're my brother, so I suppose I've little choice," Callista sighed dramatically, as the undertones sailed over her head. "Even if you are a buttknuckle."

"Buttknuckle?" Alec choked out. "What exactly is a buttknuckle?"

"No idea. After a century in captivity, it appears your sister has decided to adapt to the modern era by mastering the fine art of western slang." Luca rolled his eyes. "My advice is to just go with it without requesting an explanation. Trust me, it isn't worth the resultant headache."

Callista stuck her tongue out in her husband's direction. His face softened and assumed a tender expression Tessa never thought to glimpse on the usually taciturn warrior. The aloof and indifferent *Defensori* was clearly and completely captivated by his bride.

"Well, now everyone's been introduced, and we've established your brother is, indeed, a buttknuckle, I think it's time for you to have a nice cup of tea and get some rest, young lady," Madge announced from the doorway. "Won't you join us, Tessa? It's been a rough couple of days for you, as well. You must be exhausted."

Callista's large, blue eyes, so like her brother's,

immediately welled up. Stepping free of Alec, she threw her arms around Tessa, who instinctively stiffened in surprise.

"Here I am ranting like a spoiled child when you've so recently suffered such a tragic loss. What you must be thinking of me! I am so, so sorry," she sobbed.

Looking to Alec for help, and gaining nothing but a shrug in return, Tessa awkwardly patted the other woman's shoulder and glanced helplessly in Luca's direction.

"She's a bit emotional these days." Luca bit back a smile.

"Jeckyll and Hyde springs to mind," Alec muttered.

"She's entitled." Madge pried her daughter away from Tessa and tucked the weeping girl against her side. She reached out with her free hand and snagged Tessa's sleeve, efficiently moving the three of them as a single unit in the direction of the door. "Now, come along and have some tea. You too, Contessa. I swear, if men were the ones forced to endure childbirth, the race would be extinct."

"Oh, but I…we…" Tessa glanced at the desk and widened her eyes in Alec's direction as his mother steamrolled her from the room.

"Mom's right. You've had a rough couple of days. Go ahead and relax for a while. We'll figure this out later. I need to talk to Luca about a few things, anyway."

Luca waited until the door snicked closed behind the women before turning to Alec with an arched brow. "What the hell is going on?"

"I hoped maybe you could tell me. Barachiel left

me this." Alec indicated the materials on the desk with a sweep of his arm. "You're the one who mentioned *Djinn*. I've heard of them, of course, but have no experience in that area."

"Actually, I meant what was going on with you and Tessa, but we'll go with Barachiel's unfinished business if you prefer."

"Barachiel asked me to stand by her through this." Alec cleared his throat and moved back to the desk, unable to meet Luca's gaze. "You know as well as I she has no one else. I'd be an unfeeling jerk to not to be there for her, wouldn't I?"

"Undoubtedly." Luca shrugged off the lightweight black jacket, revealing the daggers tattooed on his forearms, and tossed it on a chair. Then he moved to stand beside Alec and regard the materials on the desktop. "Pity that wasn't your attitude ten years ago. Would have saved me a lot of trouble. I'm as susceptible as the next man to a beautiful woman in distress, you know. But, it can make for a sticky situation when the woman is another man's wife."

"It was *you*?" Alec forced out through clenched teeth as every muscle in his body seized into tight knots. "*You* were the man who brought Tessa home that night?"

"Well, it sure as hell wasn't you, was it?" As Luca reached to pick up a map, Alec's fist slammed into his brother-in-law's jaw with a sickening crack. The silver angel sailed over the desk, hitting the tile floor on the other side with a thud. Massaging his chin as he levered himself into a seated position, he then reached around to the back of his head. His eyes widened, then narrowed as his fingers came away streaked with blood.

He climbed unsteadily to his feet, his eyes fixed on Alec. Alec moved around the desk, seeing the dagger gripped in Luca's fist through a red haze of fury.

"How dare you take advantage of my wife?" With a growl, he grabbed the front of Luca's black T-shirt in one fist, and pulled back his other arm to strike again, barely aware Luca released the dagger and let it clatter to the floor.

"*Diavolo*! Have you lost your mind?" Luca shoved hard with both hands against Alec's chest, knocking him off balance, then twisted free and stepped back out of range. "I've done a lot of things I'm not proud of in my long life, but sleeping with your wife is not among them."

"She admitted it, and... I saw you." Nostrils flaring, Alec lowered his head like a bull preparing to charge, and regarded Luca steadily.

"If she claimed anything happened between us, she lied to you. Maybe you should give some thought as to why she felt the need. And if you interpreted comfort as passion, then you lied to yourself. Either way, not my problem." Luca tugged his shirt back into place. "But, I'll give you a piece of advice. Lying to yourself? Bad idea. Damages your trust in yourself, and colors everything in your life. Believe me, I know." Bending to retrieve the dagger, he slapped the weapon against his forearm, where it dissolved back into his tattoo. He straightened to his full height of six and half feet and regarded Alec with an icy expression that caused more than one *Fallen* to turn tail and run without ever putting up a fight. "Be thankful I love your sister. The last time a man cold-cocked me, the argument concluded with his entrails littering the floor."

"But, she said…" Alec trailed off and raked a shaky hand through his hair, replaying that awful night in his mind, struggling to recall Tessa's exact words through the vortex of pain that always accompanied the recollection. What *had* she said? He'd been so busy wallowing in guilt and wanting to place the blame for his own failings elsewhere, he took one look at her and threw out accusations she didn't deny. But, failure to deny wasn't exactly an admission. He ignored her youth and inexperience, didn't understand how deeply he hurt her with his unintentional indifference and preoccupation. When he handed her the opportunity to strike back, why wouldn't she? What kind of man was he to become so consumed with his own devastation and self-righteous anger, he'd failed to see hers? And then he closed his mind when she later tried to explain. *You witnessed comfort that night, not passion.* Hadn't Luca just said almost the same thing? Dear God, she wasn't unfaithful, she was hurt and uncertain. Ten years later, she still tried explaining, and he still failed to hear the truth. He sucked in a deep, shuddering breath that did little to ease the ache in his chest, and blew it out again. *I am a complete jerk.*

"I jumped to conclusions."

"No kidding. And I gather it's not the first time. You should work on that."

Alec swallowed hard and nodded. "Yeah. So, I suppose I owe you an apology?"

"Clearly. Not to mention the one you owe your wife, Buttknuckle." Luca felt the back of his head again, and after determining the bleeding stopped, he combed a portion of his thick, shiny locks over the blood stiffened ones with his fingers and turned his head for Alec's inspection. "Is it covered?"

"If the *Defensori* could see you now. Luca Fiorelli, the Ice Warrior, one of the most feared and deadly *Earthbound* on the planet. The man whose very name strikes fear into the hearts of *Fallen* and *animorti* everywhere, worried about his hair." Alec moved back behind the desk and pretended to resume his inspection of the papers. "You are such a girl."

"Actually, my concern was on your behalf should your sister notice and demand an explanation for my cracked skull. And don't make the mistake of thinking my love for Callista has made me soft on any level. I'd be delighted to prove you wrong."

"I'll take your word for it." Alec looked up. "So, now we've established I am, in fact, a buttknuckle and I jumped to conclusions, care to tell me what really happened that night?"

Chapter Eleven

"Ask your wife." Luca snapped, then he stepped over to the desk and pulled the maps and the drawing toward him.

Alec leaned forward and planted his hands on the desk, interrupting Luca's view. "I'm asking you."

"You won't like what you hear." Luca straightened and crossed his arms over his chest, straining the confines of his shirt. Pressing his lips together in a tight, thin line, he lifted his chin.

"Humor me." Alec stared at the other man, working to ignore the tight roiling in his stomach and the ache in the back of his throat.

"Very well, but let's sit down, eh? It's been a long day that just keeps getting longer." Luca motioned to a pair of overstuffed green velvet upholstered armchairs chairs set in an alcove in front of a curved triple window on either side of a mahogany table. He settled into one, stretching his long, denim clad legs out in front of him, and indicated with a wave Alec should take the other. After indulging in a jaw cracking yawn, Luca dropped his head back to rest against the chair and closed his eyes.

"Contessa's symphonic debut was an utter triumph…" Luca began. And as he continued, Alec realized Luca was right. He didn't like what he heard. Luca's words conjured a mental picture of Tessa chatting with the patrons, dazzling the critics, saying the right things to the right people, all the while wearing a pasted on smile that never reached her eyes. Making excuses for Alec's tardiness to both acquaintances and family, and lighting up whenever the door opened, still expecting him. Turning back to face her well-earned adulation with that happy light extinguished as, time after time, he failed to appear. The ache in the back of his throat spread into his chest and became a feeling he recognized though he'd felt it only once before. The sharp, acute pain of a heart breaking into a thousand pieces. But, this time his heart didn't break because of Tessa. It broke *for* her. Just as hers must have broken that night ten years ago. And he'd been the cause. It made the agony nearly unbearable. When Luca finished, Alec propped his elbows on his knees, and dropped his head into his hands.

"She's quite an actress. Your wife fooled everyone, even those who loved her most. She hailed a cab and sent them all on their way with kisses and smiles, assuring everyone she was fine. But, I knew better. As anyone is happy to tell you, I know women. Though just for the record, I've put those days firmly behind me, and would appreciate it if you didn't mention it to your sister."

Alec picked up his head and scrubbed his hands over his face. "Calli's *Earthbound*, you idiot. She's been in your head. And don't forget the whole Giovanna affair. Trust me, she knows. She loves you anyway."

Luca cracked one eye open and nodded, the corners of his lips curving up. "Yeah, she does. Anyway, after everyone left, Tessa sent the cab away and started walking. I followed. Discreetly, of course."

"Of course." Alec mocked. Luca's eyes snapped open. He lifted his head and frowned.

"I can stop right now, you know. I'd really rather be resting with my wife."

"Sorry. Go on." Alec sat back with a sigh.

"She was distraught, crying, talking to herself. Actually, I heard quite a lot of swearing, so perhaps the conversation was directed at you." He smiled and leaned back, closing his eyes once again. "At any rate, she didn't pay attention to her direction or surroundings. Beautiful girl, all alone, dark night in London. You do the math."

Her state of disarray had been the first thing he remarked on when she walked in the door in the wee hours of the morning. But, the sin hadn't been hers. It rested squarely on his shoulders. Alec's gut knotted as a sound registering somewhere between a groan and a growl clawed its way from deep within his chest like a feral beast seeking escape.

"Oh don't worry. Any asshole foolish enough to put a hand on her drew back a stump. That particular crew won't bother anyone again. I made sure of it. I took her back to my car. I drove, she cried. Eventually, she pulled herself together and asked me to bring her home. I helped her from the car, gave her an encouraging hug, kissed her on the forehead, and sent her back to you. I suppose that's what you saw." Luca straightened in the chair and shrugged. "Clearly, had I known of your idiotic misconception, I would have told you sooner."

"Thank you for protecting her when I didn't." Alec

forcibly pushed all thoughts of what could have happened to Tessa that night to the back of his mind. His stomach churned and his knees went weak thinking about it. "So, let's recap, shall we? First, I fail to show on the biggest night of her life, then she's damn near raped, or worse, because I wasn't there to protect her. After everything, she arrives home physically battered and emotionally decimated and what does her bound mate, her husband, the other half of her soul, do? Apologize? Comfort her? Hell, no. The one person she should have been able to rely on for unconditional support and protection ripped her up one side and down the other and accused her of cheating. I'm pretty sure that adds up to three strikes. Three strikes constitutes an out. I'm out, Luca. She's only here because she's grieving, and because her father asked. She'll never forgive me."

Luca pushed himself to his feet and stretched like a large, tawny cat. Then he reached down and swatted Alec in the side of the head.

"*Madre di Dio*, am I the only one in this family who pays attention?" Luca threw his arms in the air and stalked to the door. "Of course she's grieving, but she isn't here because her father asked *her*. She's here because her father asked *you*. You could have refused, but you didn't. You stepped up to the plate. Three strikes may constitute an out, but any baseball fan worth his salt knows one out doesn't end the inning. Tessa's still hoping, still pitching, Alec. Don't be afraid to take a swing. Talk to your wife."

"That's the worst analogy for a troubled marriage I ever heard," Alec laughed, climbing stiffly to his feet.

"*E perfetto!*" Luca brought his fingertips to his lips

and kissed them. Alec rolled his eyes and shook his head. "Bah, maybe it's not perfect, but it makes the point. Blame Callista and her damned TV talk shows. She coerces me into watching with her as often as possible. I suppose if you watch them long enough, you begin to think you're Freud."

Alec laughed, remembering well his sister's fascination with television following her release from a century of captivity and isolation.

"Yeah, well you should probably stick to fighting the bad guys. Wait a minute, what about this?" Alec gestured to the desk as Luca reached for the doorknob.

"It isn't going anywhere tonight, right?"

Alec hesitated. He craved the challenge. For years, he'd lived for it, in fact. And he was damned good at it. No, it wasn't going anywhere, but that never kept him from locking himself away and diving in before, to the exclusion of everything else. *Everyone* else. And what did his single-minded determination gain him? Frustration for the evil *Fallen* who sought to use Michael's follies against him? Michael's grudging respect? A sense of personal accomplishment? Sure, along with self-imposed isolation, two shattered souls, one broken marriage, and a partridge in a freaking pear tree.

"Nope." Alec forced his attention away from the mystery littering his desk and followed Luca out the door, pulling it closed behind him. Then he headed in the direction of the kitchen and Tessa. "Not going anywhere."

The vague sense of disappointment he felt on finding his mother alone in the kitchen caught Alec by surprise. Madge looked up from her fashion magazine with a smile.

"The girls have gone upstairs to have a rest. Honestly, they're both so exhausted, I'm not sure which of them to worry about more." Her brows drew together, pleating her forehead. "Callista is anxious about the birth, feeling awkward and unattractive, while Tessa teeters on the brink, suppressing her grief, and feeling as though she has no place here. I've done what I could to reassure them both, but frankly, I don't know if anything got through to either of them."

"Perhaps you aren't the one they need reassurance from," Luca observed, helping himself to a cup of coffee from the large stainless pot simmering on the stove, then pouring a second at Alec's affirmative nod in his direction.

"Perhaps not," Madge sighed, closing the magazine and pushing her cup away. "But, really Luca, I know Calli has you, but now Barachiel is gone, who does Contessa have? No one, that's who."

"She has me," Alec whispered to himself.

"What's that, dear?" His mother's expression brightened considerably. He tossed back a slug of the steaming coffee Luca plunked down in front of him, scalding his tongue. He set the cup slowly and carefully on the table, cleared his throat, and tried again.

"I said Tessa has me."

"Does she, dear?" Her eyes widened. "I didn't realize. I thought you'd washed your hands of her after..." Madge lowered her voice and glanced at Luca, who hid a smirk behind his cup. "well, *you know*."

"There wasn't another man," Alec muttered, taking another sip without thinking. He swore and slammed the cup back on the table. "I was...wrong."

"Of course you were." His mother patted his arm.

"What do you mean, 'of course you were'? Are you saying you *knew* I was wrong?"

"That girl loved you, Alec. Completely. She could no more betray you, than cut out her own heart. And of course, she told her father everything. I made it a point to keep in touch with Barachiel over the years, even if you didn't."

"Well, why in the hell didn't you say something, Mother?" He exploded, jumping to his feet. The chair clattered backwards, skidding across the tile floor. "You didn't think maybe that was need to know information?"

"If you couldn't recognize it on your own, you weren't ready to know. You wouldn't have believed me, and you certainly wouldn't have welcomed my meddling."

"I wouldn't have welcomed your meddling?" Alec repeated slowly, shaking his head. "Yet, you and Barachiel and Michael found it perfectly acceptable to scheme behind my back and concoct a plan to force us together under circumstances you knew neither of us could refuse? You manipulated me, all of you, plain and simple."

"Don't go all self-righteous indignation on me, young man. Would you rather be right? Or would you rather be with your wife?" his mother protested, as color flooded her face. "You and Tessa were both too stubborn to make the first move, well…Barachiel and I decided it wouldn't hurt to give you both a little push. Obviously, Barachiel wanted Tessa close these last months, but he sacrificed his own needs to ensure her future. With you. She loves you, Alec."

Alec jerked his head around at the sound of a strangled gasp. Pale and trembling, Tessa stood poised in the doorway.

"Tess…" Alec started around the table, but she held up a hand to stop him.

"I came down for a drink. I…didn't mean to eavesdrop. But, since I couldn't help overhearing, Madge is right. I do love you, Alec. And I understand now it was childish and unrealistic expecting one hundred percent of your attention one hundred percent of the time. But, I sure as hell deserved more than ten percent of it ninety-five percent of the time. I hoped you arrived at the same realization about why…" Tessa blinked rapidly, her throat muscles working visibly as she swallowed. Then she coughed and lifted her chin. "God knows I threw enough hints. Just for the record, picking up on subtlety is not your strong point. At any rate, I'm sorry you were tricked. Consider yourself absolved of any responsibility where I'm concerned. Loving you cost me everything. Even the final precious days I could have spent with my father. I'll always love you, but one person can't fight a battle for two. Maybe it really is time to cut our losses."

And then she disappeared.

Chapter Twelve

Tessa pressed a hand hard against her chest, as though she could hold together the fractured pieces of her heart. Every beat stabbed with the exquisite sting of a knife's blade. When she pulled her palm away, she half expected to find it sliced bloody from the jagged shards. She wondered how something already shattered produced such intense pain. But, deep down she knew. She'd foolishly allowed hope, such an insidious and deceptive monster, to sneak in and begin mending the cracks. And now her heart broke all over again. She dared to believe in the ridiculous notion love could conquer all. Or conquer enough, anyway. Except love didn't bring Alec barreling back into her life. Parental manipulation, heaped with a healthy sense of duty and obligation, sucked him in. She never heard him use that tone with his mother, so clearly he wasn't happy about it. She waited too long, allowed the wounds to fester, forging a river of hurt too deep to cross. There didn't seem to be a point in sticking around. So, after dropping her backpack and her mother's wedding box at the flat, she found herself here.

Shading her sensitive, tear-swollen eyes against the glare of the setting sun, Tessa tilted her head back and regarded the imposing façade of the *Castel Sant'Angelo*. The ticket office closed hours ago, but Tessa didn't come for a tour. She came seeking

Michael.

Working her way through the crowds meandering in the darkening square in front of the *Castel*, Tessa maneuvered around the side nearest the *Parco Adriano*, hoping to find a spot to fade inside the walls unobserved. According to legend, in the sixth century, Michael the Archangel appeared atop the mausoleum, sheathing his sword as a sign the plague ravaging the city had ended. She couldn't help thinking it would be damned convenient if the elusive Archangel had a sudden urge to make an appearance on the roof right about now. Though Michael and her father had been close friends, she'd never been to the *Castel*. She didn't have the faintest idea where to begin looking for him once she gained entry to the massive, maze-like structure.

Keeping to the shadows cast by the massive stone wall, Tessa looked around, saw no one watching, then allowed her body to dissolve. She reformed inside the front entrance, near a set of metal stairs descending to the lower level where the ramp winding to the top began. To her left was the ticket office, its slick, glass front looking incongruous amidst the ancient walls. Assuming Michael wouldn't be lounging inside counting the day's receipts, she clambered down the stairs, and started up the long, curving Roman ramp. She tread carefully, nearly turning her ankle more than once on the uneven surface, the passage dimly lit only by small, regularly spaced lights set high above the floor.

She didn't spare a glance at the second floor storerooms once containing oil and wheat, or the dark, eerie cells that were remnants of a time when the castle served as a prison. She blindly bypassed the myriad of antiquities set into niches in the damp stone walls. Climbing with speed and determination, Tessa's heart pounded and her legs shook by the time she reached the Courtyard of the Angel designed by Michelangelo for Pope Julius II. Artfully arranged pyramids of round, reproduction stone ammunition lined the walls. Believing she must surely have reached the top, Tessa's shoulders sagged when she noticed staircases on either side leading to yet another level. She couldn't remember the last time she'd been so bone weary. Stopping to catch her breath, she closed her eyes and opened her mind, sending Michael a message on the mental frequency used by *Earthbound*. Though not *Earthbound* herself, she enjoyed the same telepathic abilities by virtue of her paternal *Principalitie* heritage. While waiting to see if he would respond, she paused to admire the marble statue of the Archangel with its great, bronze wings, now green with age, which stood in the center of the courtyard surveying all who passed with a permanently imperious expression.

"Uncanny likeness, wouldn't you say?"

Tessa jumped in surprise, then spun to face the imposing figure of Michael. The nearly seven foot tall Archangel, with an equally impressive wingspan, approached from the foot of the staircase to her left, illuminating the darkening courtyard with a fantastic, golden light.

"I could probably make a more accurate assessment if I hadn't just been permanently blinded. Maybe you could tone it down a bit?" Tessa smiled as he continued to approach, his massive wings bending and folding with dizzying speed until they disappeared completely, his glow fading away as quickly. Yes, da Montelupo captured Michael's youthful attractiveness well, but upon closer inspection, the resemblance ended. Though immortally beautiful, there was nothing boyish or carefree in the haunted shadows reflected in the living Archangel's eyes.

"Better?" He opened his arms, and she stepped into them, the top of her head barely reaching his massive chest.

"Much. It's been too long. How are you?"

Michael grasped her shoulders and pulled her away slightly, gazing intently into her face.

"Better than you, I expect. You're too thin, and you look like hell."

"And you're as charmingly unfiltered as ever. Give me a break, it's been a rough few days."

"Undoubtedly. Would a nice glass of Chianti make you feel better?"

"Unlikely," Tessa sighed. "On the other hand, I doubt it will make me feel worse."

"My thoughts exactly," Michael chuckled, then wrapped his arms around her and faded them both to his hidden quarters deep within the *Castel.*

Releasing her, Michael moved away to a side table, and as he poured, Tessa's eyes roamed over the sumptuous room decorated in the Renaissance style. She recognized Raphael's hand in the gloriously colorful frescoes decorating the plastered walls and coffered ceiling. As Michael returned to her side and held out a goblet of the deep, red wine, she shook her head at the incongruity of the seventy-inch flat screen television occupying the space between two enormous paintings—one depicting the beheading of John the

Baptist and the other, the martyrdom of San Sebastiano—and the oversized leather sectional dominating the center of the room.

"I see you're really roughing it here in this enormous pile of stone. Does it occur to you these works of genius should be shared with the public?"

"The public has quite enough to see. There are over fifty museums in the vicinity of Rome, alone. They'll hardy suffer for lack of my few treasured things. So what brings you to my humble abode?" He yanked his phone from the inside pocket of his jacket, glanced at the display, and smiled. Then he waved an arm in the direction of the sofa, indicating she should have a seat. He perched on the arm as she settled into the center.

"There is nothing humble about your abode, and we both know humility has never been a virtue of its solitary resident, either."

"True, but the heavy burden of leadership should come with some perks. And you didn't answer my question." He brought the wine to his lips and regarded her steadily over the rim of the glass.

"I suspect you already know. You knew he was dying, Michael. Why didn't you contact me?"

"Because he asked me not to." He drained his glass and set it on the end table. Then he climbed to his feet and moved to the window, giving her his back. "I didn't agree with his decisions, but as his friend, I had no choice but to respect them. In much the same way he, as your father, had no choice but to respect yours. Even when he thought you were dead wrong."

"He never said he thought I was wrong," Tessa mumbled, the leather creaking in protest as she shifted her weight and gulped a hasty mouthful of wine. Of course, he'd never actually said he agreed with her, either. He'd simply listened to her myriad of excuses, allowed her to cry it out, and continued to love her unconditionally. "I'm not sure I know how to be in a world without him in it. I miss him so much already."

"I know you do. And I also know you think you have to be strong, but grief isn't weakness, Contessa, it's the price of loving someone enough to feel their loss. Heartache is grim and uncomfortable, a dark room where no one wants to stay. The reality is, it never truly ends, but it does change. You don't get over it, you learn to live around it. In time. Gradually the light returns. You will be whole again, but you'll never be the same. I believe Barachiel hoped if you had Alec, that light would return sooner, and it would hurt less to let him go."

"Well, it didn't. It simply handed me one more loss to mourn. Alec knows, you see. He knows all about how you and my father and Madge schemed to bring us together. He resents being manipulated." And no doubt resented her as the cause, niggled a tiny voice in the back of her brain. Tessa drained her glass and set it on the coffee table. The she took a deep breath, shoved her heavy mass of hair away from her face wishing she'd remembered to tie it up, and rose unsteadily to her feet. "Which brings me to the reason for my visit. I've come to set him free."

"Really?" Michael crossed his arms over his broad chest, straining the seams of his custom tailored shirt, and arched a brow, inviting her to continue. Tessa twisted her fingers together in front of her and focused her attention on the wall just over his left shoulder.

"I blamed you for a very long time, you know. You

waved your angelic toys under his nose and convinced him they were out there waiting to create havoc if they came into *Fallen* hands. Then you dared him to find them, certain he couldn't resist the challenge. And you were right."

"There was no better *Earthbound* for the job. Alec is blessed with an extraordinary talent and intellect."

"Yes, he is. Among other things. Do you know, even after fifty years together, every time I looked at him, the love I felt took my breath away? I wondered what I could possibly have done in my short life to deserve him. But, as time passed and he became increasingly obsessed with the work, I found myself fighting for his attention. I began to doubt myself, doubt his feelings for me." Tessa shrugged. "I was young, insecure. It's not much of an excuse, but it's all I've got. It's never easy to see beyond your own pain and view your actions from someone else's perspective. It's taken me years, but it's excruciatingly enlightening. It forced me to grow up. The hard way."

"I've never met anyone who found an easy way." The corners of Michael's lips twitched.

"Well, maybe you could pass it along to the powers in charge…there should be, because the alternative really sucks." Tessa lips curled up reluctantly in return. "At any rate, Alec was wrong to treat me as an afterthought, but I realize now it was unintentional— unconscious. My retaliation, on the other hand, was deliberate. And cruel. Perhaps unforgivably so."

"Few things in life are unforgivable. Did you walk in the door that night with a well thought out plan to convince him you'd been unfaithful?"

"Of course not. I walked in the door hoping there'd

be some miraculous, earthshattering reason Alec failed me on one of the most important nights of my life. Instead, I got anger and accusations. I should have had the monopoly on angry and hurt that night. I know I looked a mess, but he never even asked what happened. I'd never given him any reason to doubt me. Yet, he so easily jumped to the worst conclusion. Why?"

"Guilt."

Tessa's heart kicked her hard in the ribs as she slowly turned to face a man emerging from the darkened interior of the walnut cabinet at the back of the room. Alec.

Chapter Thirteen

Alec stepped free of the cabinet serving as the hidden entrance from the public areas of the *Castel* to Michael's quarters, and left the door hanging open. He'd been frantic when he materialized at the flat in the *Borgo* and discovered her backpack and her mother's wedding box, but no Tessa. With no signs of a struggle, he discarded his initial panicked thought the *animorti* had returned. Where could she be? After discarding one idea after another, he could think of only one other place in Rome she might go. Heart racing, hands trembling, he fired off a text. When his query to the commander of the *Defensori* received a smiley face emoji in response, he knew he'd guessed correctly. She'd gone to Michael. Still, Alec's pulse didn't resume a normal rhythm until he'd stepped into the walnut cabinet in the Pope Paul III treasure room, endured a brain scrambling spin, and clapped eyes on Tessa as he silently opened the door on the other side. Then, just when he remembered how to breathe, his gut dropped into his boots when she announced she'd come to set him free. Like hell. He squared his shoulders and pressed his lips together. Generous of her, but so not happening.

"What?" She breathed, a hand fluttering to her throat.

"You heard me. We need to talk." Alec locked eyes

with Tessa, holding his breath until she finally closed her eyes and nodded.

"A moment if you please, Your Grace?" He glanced at Michael and jerked his chin in the direction of a door leading to another room.

"My, my, aren't we formal today? And, since it seems to have escaped your notice..." Michael poked his index finger in the air and twirled it in a circle. "I live here."

"Your point?"

"Find somewhere else to grovel to your wife and don't let the door hit you in the ass." The Archangel turned his attention to Tessa, pulled her close, and dropped a kiss on the top of her fiery curls. "It was good to see you, Tess."

"Thanks for listening."

"For you, two ears, no waiting...anytime, *cara*. Don't stay away so long next time."

Tessa nodded into Michael's chest, then turned to Alec. He held out a hand. Her shoulders rose and fell as she drew in a deep breath and blew it out, then she reached and curled her fingers around his. He moved in the direction of the cabinet, but she yanked him to a stop as he tugged her toward the open door. He turned to find all color flown from her already pale face.

"What's wrong?"

"Can't we just fade out?" She whispered. "I'm not especially fond of small, enclosed places. Especially dark ones."

"Since when?"

"I don't know, exactly," Tessa gazed up at him, her confusion apparent in her expression. "I just suddenly realized I'm not."

"Michael's *sigils* recognize only his molecular signature. No one fades in or out unless they're in physical contact with him. Everyone else is forced to use the back door. Close your eyes and hold on to me. I promise it'll be fine. Trust me?" Alec lost himself in her wary blue eyes while awaiting her answer. *Trust me.* Less a question than a plea. Two words they both knew referred to much more than a two second trip through a whirling portal. The iron band squeezing his chest snapped free and fell away completely when, at last, she squeezed his fingers and took a step in the direction of the cabinet.

"Okay. Just promise you won't let me go."

"I'll never let you go." Alec shook his head with a self-deprecating smirk. Wasn't he just the master of double entendre today? Though he noticed the remark sailed right over Tessa's head. Her full attention seemed to be riveted on the dark confines of the cabinet at the moment.

Alec waited until Tessa finally made a move to enter the tight space, and lifted a foot to climb in behind her. Pressing his lips to her knuckles, he untangled their interlocked fingers.

"Wait a sec." Striding across the room, he stopped in front of the Archangel.

"What?" Michael arched a brow.

"I'll admit, the idea of the three of you conspiring behind my back really pissed me off at first, but..." Alec offered the commander a crooked grin and stuck out a hand. He couldn't miss Michael's quickly suppressed expression of surprise as he clapped his palm against Alec's in return. "Thanks. I think Tess and I can work it out from here, yeah?"

"See that you do," Michael replied in an absent tone as Alec hustled back to the wall unit and climbed in, wrapping one arm around Tessa and pulling her close. He felt her heart jump against his chest and race like a frightened rabbit's as he reached to close the door.

"Relax, I've got you."

Tessa stiffened in his arms before sagging against him with a soft sigh. Alec wondered at her reaction until he realized for the first time in ten years, without a second thought or a moment of hesitation, he'd willingly opened his mind to her and communicated on their own private mental pathway.

"Silly man, you've always had me. Try not to forget it again."

No, he wouldn't forget. He'd been so hell bent on demonstrating he could wage war against the *Fallen* just as well as his brother, he'd lost sight of something infinitely more important. Something infinitely more precious. Specifically, the woman currently clinging to him with a grip strong enough to fracture his ribs. Chuckling, he gently pried her arms free and repositioned them where they were less likely to cause damage. His talk show obsessed sister would probably accuse him of suffering from middle child syndrome. And just maybe she'd be right. Neither the lauded first-born, nor the coddled baby, he was the middle child struggling to stand out, to prove his worth. But, the only one who'd required proof was Alec himself. And without ever realizing it, he'd let it color his perceptions and impact every aspect of his life. Until now. Because now he understood he'd always been important to those who were important to him. He didn't need to be a hero. He only needed to be himself. Whether he was a *Defensori*, a super sleuth, or a street sweeper. It made no difference to his family. It didn't matter to Tessa. He was enough.

"Hey, Michael?" he called, poking his head out of the half closed door.

"Yeah?" The Archangel glanced up with a frown.

"I quit."

Alec closed the door, plunging them into darkness, while laughing out loud at the look on Michael's face. Then he wrapped both arms around Tessa and pulled her close as she buried her face in his chest and the cabinet launched into a dizzying spin.

The instant Alec opened the door on the other side of the portal, Tessa tore free of his embrace and scrambled from the cabinet. Bent nearly double, her hair tumbling forward in a thick, wavy curtain hiding her face, she braced her hands on her knees, drawing in great, gulping mouthfuls of air. Uncertain how to help her, Alec placed a tentative hand on her back and stroked rhythmic, comforting circles until at last she straightened and pushed her hair back. Damp wisps clung to her cheeks and forehead and her color had faded from pale to non-existent.

"I'm okay, now," she croaked. "I'm okay."

"You sure as hell don't look okay." Alec pressed his lips together, a stone of unease settling in his gut. He pulled her into his arms, one hand smoothing the wayward tendrils out of her eyes. "You've never been claustrophobic before. When did this start?"

"I have no idea." Tessa shook her head, gazing up at him with wide, worried eyes. "I did have some anxious moments getting on the plane, which never happened before, but I chalked it up to lack of sleep and worry for my father. It didn't even come close to this. As soon as that door closed, I felt alone, imprisoned, with an overwhelming urgency to escape. In my head, I knew you were right there holding me, but I couldn't feel you. It was just me, alone in the dark, surrounded by whispers, overcome with desperation and despair."

"Tess, it lasted three seconds, five tops."

"I know." She dropped her forehead to his chest and nodded. "I don't understand it either. It seemed like forever, like it would never end. It felt like one of my nightmares, except I couldn't wake up."

"Well, if this is how they affect you, let's be thankful you don't have them very often."

"Actually, over the last several years, they've gotten more and more frequent." She turned her head and rested her cheek over his heart with a sigh. "I don't know why. But, I'd left you, moved away from my father. While I enjoyed the work, loved the students, I formed no real relationships there. Maybe the increased nightmares were my subconscious reaction to my self-imposed isolation."

"I had no idea they were this bad. I'm so sorry."

"Don't be." She propped her chin on his chest and looked up at him with a faint smile. At least her color was returning. "It isn't your fault. I've had them for years."

Maybe the nightmares themselves weren't his fault, but how many nights did she wake up in this condition, alone in the dark, while he buried his nose in his research? Yet, she'd never complained. Just one more kick in the ass he deserved. It seemed there was no end to the levels on which he'd failed her.

"I know back there I said we need to talk. I'm not sure that's entirely accurate. I think it's more a case of I need to talk and you need to listen. C'mon." Alec pressed his lips to Tessa's still moist curls and set her away from him. Then he linked his fingers through hers and guided her around the enormous chests occupying the center of the Treasury Room, and out into the more ornate rooms of Alessandro Farnese, Pope Paul III.

"This room is incredible," Tessa gasped, craning her neck to take it all in as Alec hurried her along. Decorated in frescoes and stucco relief, depictions of Michael and Hadrian monitored their progress through the space from opposite sides of the vaulted ceiling.

"Yeah." He paused to allow her to enjoy it, thankful the dark shadows haunting her eyes appeared to be fading. "See that?"

He brought his head close to hers and pointed to an enormous crest featuring the fleur-de-lis surrounded by unicorns prominently situated in the center of the ceiling. "The Farnese coat of arms. With Michael on one end of the room and the Emperor Hadrian on the other, it was Paul III's way of proclaiming he'd single-handedly brought together classical and Christian tradition. In his opinion, at least. The theme in all of the frescoes commissioned by Paul III is he's the heir of the ancient emperors and the savior of Rome."

"Hmm, really modest guy," Tessa smiled. "And the woman seated with the unicorn below it?"

"A symbol for chastity. Of course, Alessandro Farnese, later Paul III, received his appointment to the College of Cardinals by virtue of his younger sister's affair with Alexander VI, the Borgia pope. And since Farnese, himself, claimed at least one mistress, along with multiple children, including a grandson who also rose to the office of pope, the irony is inescapable." Alec shrugged. "Still, he was a dedicated patron of the arts. Everyone employed nepotism to advance the power and fortunes of the family in those days. It was a different time."

"Indeed," Tessa whispered. Alec glanced down and his heart lurched at her unmistakable exhaustion. He'd planned to take her up to the roof, to present her with the wondrous, panoramic vista of the Eternal City at night, hoping her delight in the view would work in his favor when he spilled his guts. And there he went, making it all about him again.

"Come here." He coaxed in a gentle voice. In the blink of an eye, he released her hand and scooped her up against his chest. Seconds later, she lay curled in his arms on the sofa in the *Borgo* flat.

"Mmm, this is nice," Tessa murmured in a sleepy voice. "Thank you."

She shifted her position, grinding her softly rounded bottom into his groin. A very specific part of his anatomy jumped to attention, calling to mind exactly how much nicer it could be. Alec dropped his head back against the sofa with a barely suppressed groan. Reminding himself of Tessa's exhaustion, the fact they hadn't really talked yet, and his resolution to start putting her needs ahead of his own, he shifted uncomfortably and counted the cracks in the ancient plaster ceiling.

"Alec?" She mumbled over a yawn. "Did I hear you tell Michael you quit your job?"

"Go to sleep, Tess. We'll talk later."

"You can't quit your job, Alec. You love that job."

Yeah, he loved the job. But, he didn't love the person he became in its pursuit. Seeing Tessa again didn't just forced him to consider the state of his marriage, it compelled him to take a good, hard look at himself. He saw a self-absorbed, glory seeking asshole concerned with no one's needs except his own. He took the exquisite, singular, gifted woman in his arms for granted, assuming in his arrogance she would always be there, content to wait until he had time to spare. In short, he became a blind, unfeeling caricature of Alec McAllister, a shadow of the man Tessa married, someone he barely recognized. He wasn't that man. He didn't want to be that man, not again. Not ever. Yeah, he loved the job, but without Tessa, even the victories rang hollow. Because, despite the I-don't-give-a-rat's-ass attitude he adopted since she left, nothing meant anything without her. Her soft, even breathing indicated she'd already fallen asleep. She wouldn't hear. But, he had to say it. Because now he once again found himself, he found his truth.

"I love you more."

Chapter Fourteen

Tessa woke to skin warmed by ribbons of sunlight filtering through the slats of the long, wooden shutters, and the rich aroma of freshly brewed coffee. Feeling more rested and refreshed than she had in what seemed like forever after a deep and surprisingly dreamless sleep, she stretched like a contented cat. Still wearing her clothes from the day before, she swung her legs over the side of the sofa. Her bare feet struck the smooth, cool tile just as Alec appeared in the doorway of the small, but well-equipped kitchen of the flat. He balanced two cups of coffee in one hand and dangled a paper bag in the other. His gaze roamed over her in silence, then he cleared his throat and strode into the room.

"Morning."

"Hi." Tessa combed her fingers through her sleep tangled hair and flipped it behind her shoulders. "Dare I hope that's breakfast? I'm starving."

"Uh, yeah. I popped downstairs and picked up some *cornetti.* Luca claims Giovanna's are the best in the city. Since I don't remember the last time either of us had anything to eat, I figured they could taste like rolled cardboard and it wouldn't make much difference."

He plunked everything down on the small, round dining table set in front of the window and pulled out a chair, waving her into it. Tessa perched on the edge and pulled the bag toward her, while Alec busied himself throwing open the shutters, allowing the golden morning light to fill the room. The window gave him slightly more difficulty, but at last, with a screech of protest, the warped, wooden frame lost the battle. He jerked up the sash and the industrious, early morning sounds of *Borgo Pio* filtered in from below. Boasting clean accommodations, restaurants, and souvenir shops dealing in everything from lavish ecclesiastical regalia to bobble-head figures of the pope, the small street in the old neighborhood near the Vatican teemed with people from morning until night.

Tessa bit into the crisp, croissant-like pastry, still warm from the oven and decided Luca was right. This Giovanna had a way with dough. She washed a bite of the flaky roll down with a mouthful of dark, fragrant *espresso* and sighed. Alec flitted from one pile of boxes, books, and paintings to another, repositioning and rearranging them. Her father's things occupied nearly every available space in the small flat, and no amount of reshuffling would bring order to the chaos. She didn't relish the thought of going through everything, but it would have to be done. Eventually. Maybe she could simply maintain the flat as a storage unit?

"You may as well sit down and eat. You're fighting a losing battle," she observed over the rim of her cup. *I love you more.* Did Alec truly utter those words? Or was it a trick played by her imagination somewhere in the twilight world between wakefulness and sleep? Once, she believed him giving up his work was exactly what she wanted. Childish, selfish, craving nothing less than his all. Now, the idea stabbed at her conscience like a splinter wedged beneath a broken fingernail. Love required compromise, but it shouldn't require complete sacrifice of one's needs for the other. Wasn't that how they'd descended to this particular level of hell to begin with?

"So, you said we needed to talk," Tessa prompted, taking a deep breath and helping herself to another *cornetto*. Then she spread a napkin on the table and set one at Alec's place, while he stepped into the kitchen to wash the dust from his hands. He returned and pulled out the other chair.

"If I remember correctly, I said I need to talk and you need to listen." He raised the cup to his lips and took a quick sip. Then set it back in front of him and broke off one end of the pastry. Instead of popping it in his mouth, he crumbled it between his fingers, and stared at her across the short width of the table.

"Okay. We can start there, I guess. So talk. I'm listening." She'd been waiting to listen for ten years.

"I know Luca brought you home that night."

"Because he told you."

"Yeah. If anyone was betrayed that night, Tess, it was you, not me. I attacked out of guilt, you defended out of pain. I know it hardly cuts it, but I'm sorry."

"I see." Tessa placed the half eaten roll on the table and picked up her cup as the light-as-air pastry turned to dust in her mouth. She drained the cup, then pushed back from the table and climbed to her feet on rubber legs.

"What's that supposed to mean?" Alec's brows drew together and he pushed back his own chair and rose.

"It means, I see. I see you know the truth, so now you're willing to talk." Tessa's breath hitched and she gripped the back of the chair until her knuckles blanched. Her heart thudded dully against her ribs, feeling smaller and tighter with every beat. "I see Luca validating my innocence gives you a free pass to believe in it. Rather old fashioned to require a man to attest to a woman's chastity, isn't it? I *had* hoped you'd reached the conclusion on your own."

"I think maybe I did. But, projecting my anger on you over the years became second nature. I guess I found it a whole lot more comfortable than facing the truth."

"Well, far be it from me to disturb your comfort zone." Tessa released the chair and wrapped her arms around herself, her fingers digging into the sides of her waist as though she could physically hold herself together. Funny, she'd envisioned this conversation completely differently. Alec shook his head like a baffled lion and stepped toward her, gripping her shoulders and pulling her against him when she tried to step away. Pinching her lips together to keep them from trembling, she lifted her chin, and forced herself to look him defiantly in the eye.

"Look, Tess, I'm not very good at this, okay? The truth is, I've always known where to place the blame for what happened that night. I knew you'd be upset with me, justifiably so. Still, I arrogantly took for granted you'd forgive and forget, like every other time I'd thoughtlessly let you down. But, that night I crossed a line. I hurt you and made you feel unimportant and insignificant one too many times. And I knew it. If you *had* sought comfort elsewhere, I could hardly blame you for seeking the respect and affection you deserved from me."

"But, you *did* blame me." She tore her gaze from his deep blue eyes, and focused on the front of his black tee, instead. "You cut yourself off, and you blamed me. For ten years. If my father didn't die…" Her voice cracked. "I'd be in Kentucky and you'd still be somewhere blaming me."

"Then I guess we should be grateful for meddlesome parents, after all," Alec sighed, releasing his painful grip on her shoulders and folding her into his arms. Tessa allowed her hands to drop to her sides, but continued to hold herself taut and slightly away. "And for the record, I didn't blame you for ten years. Maybe seventy-two hours, tops. Then I forced myself to face facts, as unpleasant as they were. Yeah, I was hurt and angry, but I loved you. The blame was more mine than yours. I knew we could find a way to get past it. But, by then you were already gone."

"And you never tried to find me."

"I thought you made your choice. And considering the pain I'd already caused you, I decided it was kinder to let you go. I'm so sorry. If I could go back in time and do things differently, I would."

Tessa swallowed hard and glanced up through her lashes. There was tenderness in his eyes, and behind it, a flash of desire so raw it made her gasp. Her heart tripped, then kicked into a sprint. Her breath caught in her throat as an answering heat sparked in her core, the warmth racing through her body like a runaway train. Fisting her hands in the fabric at his waist, she tipped her head back to meet his gaze fully, ignoring the tears escaping the corners of her eyes and streaming down her face.

"I accused you of failing to fight for me, for us. But, I failed, too." Her words came out in a throaty whisper. "I could have stayed, waited you out, and tried to explain. Instead, I ran away. Then I stayed away, sure I'd pushed you too far to ever forgive me."

"Forgiveness was never an issue. I struggled with forgetting." His voice was thick and hoarse. Burying his hands in the hair on either side of her head, he brushed the moisture from her cheeks with his thumbs, then traced their path with his lips.

"Maybe we shouldn't forget. Either of us. Maybe we should always remember that pain, so we never become those two impetuous, desperate, foolish people again. So we never repeat their mistakes." Tessa turned her cheek into his palm.

"I got so caught up in proving my own value, I destroyed your faith in yours. And you've always been worth at least ten of me. I promise you, it won't happen again. I love you, Tessa. I've been half alive without you. Come home."

"Home isn't a place, remember? It's a choice." Tessa reached to stroke back the stubborn curl tumbling over his forehead, then slid her hands up the hard planes of his chest and locked them behind his neck, pulling his dark head down to hers. "And I choose you, Alec."

"I'll always choose you." She opened her mind and he responded in kind, allowing their thoughts and feelings to intertwine. She made no attempt to hide the jagged pain of their separation, but feeling his distress, she soothed it with the balm of a love strong enough to swallow the hurt and remain undiminished. Alec's eyes

shimmered with moisture, and she knew he'd gotten the message. No matter where she'd been or what roof stood over her head, he'd always been her home. He always would be.

Still clasping her face in his hands, Alec captured her mouth with a slow, exquisitely gentle kiss. He didn't rush, his lips and tongue coaxing and teasing, and time slid away as though it didn't exist. When he raised his head at last, heated passion mingled with hesitant uncertainty in his eyes. Tessa melted into him and pulled his head back to hers. Her lips opened readily to his seeking tongue, and as he stroked and plundered, she answered his greedy kiss with one of her own. Thankful for the strength of his arms around her as her bones dissolved, Tessa sagged against him. Slipping her hands under the hem of his shirt, the heated skin of his flat stomach twitched in response to her light touch. Her hands skimmed higher, nails deliberately scraping over his sensitive nipples, and his heartbeat accelerated against her palm. The breath rasped in and out of his lungs. He looped an arm around her waist and hauled her against him, his mouth slanting over hers with a feral growl, as though he intended to devour her. Tessa could totally get on board with that. Sliding her hands from his neck to wrap around his waist and press her body more intimately to his, she felt him already rock hard and pulsing. Her stomach muscles tightened and a rush of moist heat erupted between her thighs. Alec tore his lips from hers, swept aside the heavy curtain of her hair, and began to work his magic along the column of her throat. With a soft moan, Tessa automatically tipped her head back to allow him access. While his lips and tongue relearned the contours of her ear, his fingers dove into the waistband of her jeans and splayed across her buttocks, kneading and caressing, his teasing touch so close, yet still much too far away from where she craved it most. He lifted, Tessa jumped, and her ankles locked around his waist as he staggered in the direction of the bedroom.

"Sofa's closer," Tessa panted.

"And not nearly sturdy enough. I plan to make love to every last inch of you until you scream."

A shiver rolled over her from head to toe as he dropped her on the bed and whipped off his shirt, tossing it in the corner. The ache of arousal swept through her body, a heated flush increasing in intensity in direct proportion to every inch of skin revealed to her hungry gaze. By the time he yanked off his boots, shoved his jeans to his ankles, and kicked them across the room, she managed to wriggle out of most of her own clothes. Only her lacy black panties remained when he finally reached for her.

She squirmed as he hooked his thumbs in the sides of her panties and shimmied them down her hips, following their slow, torturous path with kisses as soft as summer rain. He slipped them over her ankles and tossed them aside. Then he began a slow crawl back up her body, teasing his stubble-rough jaw along the tender skin of her inner thighs and quivering belly. He climbed, his roving hands relearning and reclaiming the curves of her body, branding her as his with every caress. He reached for her breasts, mounding them in his big hands, and her core clenched at the hot clasp of his lips on her nipple. Tessa buried her fingers in his thick, soft curls and arched against his mouth, holding him to her. His insistent lips drew on her, while he slipped a hand between her thighs, his clever fingers igniting a wildfire that threatened to consume her. Her entire body trembled with need. He hadn't forgotten *exactly* how to drive her crazy.

"Did you expect I would?" He chuckled against her breast. She jumped, forgetting he could now read her thoughts.

"You know I love foreplay, but at the moment I'm feeling it might be overrated. I want you inside me. Now."

He dropped his head into the hollow of her throat, his shoulders slick and heaving.

"I want this time to be about you. Once I get in you, I'll never last."

"Alec, look at me," she said aloud, tugging at his hair until he exhaled loudly and lifted his head. The strain of holding a tight rein on his own need showed in the sweat peppering his brow, the dark, stormy passion blazing in his eyes, and the deep grooves carved along the sides of his lips. "This isn't our first time. And it won't be our last time. But, it sure as hell *has* been a long time." She worked a trembling hand between them and curled her fingers around his shaft. Wrapping her legs around his hips, she pressed her heels into his ass, urging his hips to hers. "I need you. Now. It doesn't matter how long it lasts. I just need to feel you inside me."

"Well, okay." He drawled, settling his hands on either side of her head. He flashed a sly, seductive grin. With slow deliberation, he lowered his head and captured her lips in a leisurely and tender kiss expressing more than words ever could. "But, only because I promised myself I'd start considering your needs ahead of my own."

Then he rocked his hips and speared into her in one long thrust. Tessa moaned and writhed beneath him as her body welcomed every last inch of him home. They moved together, their hearts, minds, and bodies melding as closely and intimately as ever. Tessa gouged her nails into the hard slab of his wide shoulders and tightened her legs around him, tilting her hips, desperate to feel even more of him. He dug his fingers into her bottom possessively, shifted his position, and drove even deeper, as their bodies achieved perfect understanding in a language as old as time. Her eyes filled with tears as the unmistakably right sensation of the invisible ties binding them heart, mind, and soul wove back together, filling the empty gaps and repairing the frayed edges. It was almost too much. Tessa gritted her teeth and held on, as something deep and hot and aching raced toward a crescendo. She strained against him as every nerve ending in her body came alive, clamoring for attention. Features twisted in ecstasy, Alec drove into her over and over, the force of his passion lifting her from the bed. Lightning crackled through her veins, building to a storm that swept her up in a tidal wave. Then the maelstrom crashed over them both, drowning her in agonizing bliss as, with a powerful thrust and a deafening roar, Alec found his own release and filled her with the essence of his soul.

Chapter Fifteen

Alec rolled to his back, relieving Tessa of his weight. She moved with him and snuggled into his side, her ragged breaths warm and moist against his skin. She threw a leg over his thighs and draped an arm across his waist, and Alec returned to Earth slowly, quite content to never move from this place. What seemed like hours, in fact, took only minutes. Not what he intended at all, yet no less profound in its brevity. His throat and chest were thick and tight, strangling him with riot of emotions that froze his voice. His heart punched against his ribs with such force, he could barely form a coherent thought, let alone find the right words. Then he felt the tentative touch of Tessa's mind in his, and he realized words weren't necessary. They were inadequate, anyway. She knew. How did he ever allow anything to become more important than this? Alec gazed down at the magnificent creature in his arms, her shimmering blue eyes, the fiery trail of her glorious hair spilling over his arm and blazing a path across the crisp whiteness of the pillow, and marveled at his miracle. A blind man whose sight had been restored. A rebirth, a second chance, a gift he knew he didn't deserve. But, one he vowed he would never take for granted again.

"God, how I missed you," he whispered into her hair, inhaling the faint raspberry scent of her shampoo, now mingled with sweat and the musky perfume of their frantic lovemaking.

"I missed you, too." Tessa pressed her lips to his chest, then tilted her head back and gazed at him through her thick lashes, a smile curving her lips and a spark of mischief lighting her eyes. "And while that was damn good, and I love a compliment as much as the next girl, I hardly think it's necessary to address me as a deity."

Alec regarded her blankly for a moment, then burst out laughing as he discerned her meaning. He rolled to the side and pinned her beneath him. Then he smoothed her hair away from her face, and pressed his lips lightly to hers. "Sorry, I must have mistaken you for Aphrodite, my own personal goddess of beauty, desire, and love, risen from the sea and cast upon my bed. Seriously, Tess, could you be any cornier?"

"Look who's talking. Your Aphrodite? Anyway, I can't help it if I'm feeling a little corny at the moment. Corny, and happy, and...complete." She sighed and reached to cup his face. "How did we both get so far off track and then let it continue for so long?"

"I think you hit the nail on the head when you said we're two relatively intelligent people suffering from a severe case of common-sense-stupid syndrome. Of course, given the length of our lives, I figure ten years in our world is probably comparable to a separation lasting a couple of days, a week tops, in mortal terms."

"I call bullshit." She yanked a lock of his hair, then combed her fingers through it, soothing the sting. "Ten years is ten years on any terms, and it's—What's that?" She turned her head toward a persistent buzzing sound coming from the corner of the room where his jeans lay in a crumpled heap. He dropped his forehead against hers with a sigh. Apparently it was too much to hope the world would simply disappear and leave them in peace for the day.

"My phone. I knew my mother would call to check on my whereabouts sooner or later, so I turned the ringer off last night." Alec reluctantly untangled his limbs from Tessa's and climbed from the bed, immediately mourning the loss of her warmth. Scooping his jean from the floor, he fumbled through the pockets for his phone and checked the display. "Yep, two from Luca, three from Michael, and five from the woman who recently assured me she'd resigned herself to the fact her children were adults with several hundred years of life experience under their belts and who were capable of taking care of themselves."

"She's your mother. You were angry when you left, and she has no idea where you are. The woman taught you to use a spoon. A simple phone call to let her know you're okay isn't asking for much in return." Alec glanced away from the screen to where Tessa sat on the edge of the rumpled bed poking her legs through her panties. He propped a shoulder against the wall, warmth radiating throughout his body, heart drumming in his chest, captivated by the grace of her lithe form as she hopped to her feet and gathered the rest of her carelessly discarded clothes into a bundle. His eyes devoured the sweet curve of her ass swaying in the direction of the bathroom, until she turned in the doorway and planted her free hand in a fist on the delicious swell of her hip. "Also, an apology might be in order. I don't like being manipulated either, but let's face it, we weren't in any danger of making progress on our own."

"Let me get this straight. You're saying I should *thank* my mother for treating us like children and interfering?"

"We *acted* like children, Alec."

"Yeah," he exhaled his agreement on a long, resigned breath, rubbing a hand over the back of his neck. "I guess we did. So, I'll text her and let her know we're fine. And I'll apologize when I see her. Happy?"

"Happier than I thought I could be, all things considered. You'll thank her, too, right?"

"Yes, dear. Go take your shower."

"You know, I'm really liking this attentive, agreeable side of you, husband." She waggled her brows and beamed at him across the room.

"Just don't interpret it as a willingness to become hen-pecked, wife."

"Really, Alec! I am *so* not that girl." She blew him a kiss and stepped into the bathroom, pushing the door closed behind her. But, just before the latch caught, she called out a final parting shot. "Later we'll discuss this crazy idea you have about quitting your job, too."

They would like hell. There was nothing to discuss. Didn't she get it? The job caused this mess, at least in part. Alec turned his phone up, texted his mother, and tossed the device on the bed. He would find another job. Not that he needed the money, *Earthbound* lived long enough to accumulate vast wealth over centuries. Hell, look at his brother. Kassian stood to stuff an additional eight figures in his overflowing pockets as soon as he inked the deal currently in negotiation for McAllister Publishing. Alec's more modest bankroll didn't approach his older brother's affluence, but he could easily finance a small country. For a few hundred years. Maybe a nice teaching job. Easy nine-to-five, no weekends or holidays, no additional obligations save the occasional faculty dinner where he could show off his stunningly beautiful wife. Smiling at the mental picture of Tessa, resplendent in evening wear charming the pants off his fictional colleagues, he yanked on his jeans. Then he dropped his ass on the bed and grabbed a boot. His phone chimed and he picked it up and checked the screen.

Come home.

Well, apparently his mother had forgiven his bout of bad temper. Kind of an odd response, though. He shoved the phone in the pocket of his jeans. Hell, he could even apply for a couple of research grants. It would give him something to do with all that free time. He could...the boot slipped from his nerveless fingers and hit the floor. His gut cramped, then churned like a cement mixer. He hadn't even settled on a job yet and he was doing it already. Propping his elbows on his knees, he dropped his head into his hands and groaned. No, he didn't care about the money. He craved the chase. He hungered for occupation of mind like a junkie craves a drug.

Tessa bolted from the bathroom and rushed to where he sat on the bed, dropping to her knees between his legs. Wearing nothing but a towel, her long hair dripped down her back forming a rapidly expanding puddle on the tile behind her. Shit, he forgot he let her in his head. If she sensed his turmoil, then she certainly knew its cause.

"Alec?" She gently pried his fingers away from his face. "Talk to me."

"I can't." He shook his head and shot to his feet, keenly aware her wide, worried eyes tracked his restless pacing from one end of the small room to the other. He'd always considered himself a fairly good guy. Not perfect by any means, but not the thoughtless bastard he'd apparently been rocking all these years. How could he open his mouth and tell her he just had a freaking epiphany? That after all they'd been through, after finding their way back, after everything, he would inevitably destroy them again. All this sudden self-awareness shit was really getting on his last nerve.

"No, you won't," Tessa announced, climbing to her feet. "Because I won't let you."

"Don't you get it, Tess? I'm an addict and the challenge is my drug of choice. Solving the riddle, fitting the next piece of the puzzle, when I'm in the middle of it, I'm consumed. It was never the job. It was me."

"Well, you know what they say about addiction. Admitting you have a problem is half the battle." She moved to a large box in the corner labeled with her name, tore open the flaps, and withdrew a stack of neatly folded clothes. She deposited everything on a chair, then rifled through the pile, tossing clean undies, jeans, and a blue tank top on the bed.

"I don't think they have a twelve step program for this."

"Alec, you're an extremely intelligent man with a freakish curiosity that never allows your mind to rest. I love that about you. But, it's all about balance. You don't need a twelve step program. You need to set limits. Prioritize."

"And you believe I can do it?"

"I know you can." She walked across the room and stopped in front of him. "In fact, you already have."

"Right."

"No, seriously. When I came downstairs last night, you were in the kitchen having coffee with your mother and Luca."

"So?"

"So, where was the packet from my father? I'll tell you where. In the office, spread out all over the desk. A new puzzle just begging to be solved."

"That was a probably a set-up, Tess. A wild goose chase. Part of the great reunion scheme."

"Even if that's true, you didn't think so at the time. Yet, you walked away. Why?"

Alec stared down at her raised brows, the defiant, expectant expression, and found himself at a loss to understand her ardent faith in him. He thought back to the previous evening, the confrontation followed by the conversation with Luca, the mental profit-loss analysis of his work for Michael, then heading to the kitchen to find Tessa. The tightness in his chest eased as his second epiphany of the day struck. People make time for the things they choose to make time for, the *people* they choose to make time for. He'd chosen poorly in the past. This time, he got it right. He walked away. He chose her. He chose what mattered most. Tessa still believed in him. And if her faith remained intact even after the many times he'd failed, then he had no business doubting himself.

"Because the price of not learning when to walk away is too high."

"And my work here is done."

She slapped her hands against one another as

though brushing dust from her palms and took a bow.

"You've changed, Tess." Alec cocked his head to the side and regarded her curiously. More confident, more assertive, insightful, more willing to challenge him and make him see things from a point of view other than his own. He'd always seen her as someone who needed to be taken care of. By him. And he'd enjoyed her dependence on him. But now? She still loved him, still wanted him, but he wasn't so sure she needed him anymore. He didn't know how he felt about that. But, maybe loving and wanting without actually needing was a healthier situation for both of them. Still his loving, beautiful Tessa but...more.

"I grew up." She shrugged. Then she smiled, stretched up on her toes to plant a kiss on his chin, and yanked at the knotted fabric between her breasts. The towel dropped to the floor and Alec's mind went blank.

"See? Priorities. Works every time."

Alec grinned, springing at her, but coming up empty as Tessa dove for the bed, squealing with laughter. She snagged her clothes as the forward momentum carried her over to the other side. Giggling, she scrambled into panties and jeans. Alec raised a foot as though he intended to start around the bed, his grin widening when she bought the ruse and scurried back toward a chair, struggling with her bra. He disappeared before his foot struck the floor, materializing behind the chair. She backed right into him and he flinched at the icy contact of her wet hair against his bare chest. His arms came around her, pinning hers to her sides. She gasped, and whipped her head around, flinging water droplets everywhere.

"That's not fair."

"I don't have to be fair. Told you, this isn't a democracy."

"Obviously." She sniffed, tossing her head. "It's clearly a matriarchy."

"Well, you just keep telling yourself that, sweetness. I'll even humor you for the moment by playing ladies' maid." Alec released her arms and snagged the two dangling ends of her bra. He hooked the clasp, then swept her wet hair to the side and pressed his lips to the nape of her neck. "Now, stop poking the bear and get dressed." He laughed and smacked her bottom.

Tessa stuck out her lower lip and marched to the bed. She snatched at the tank top and dragged it over her head.

"Technically, it isn't teasing if I'm perfectly ready, willing, and able to follow through."

"Oh really?" he drawled. "Well, it just so happens I have every intention of letting you show me just how ready, willing, and able you are." His phone pinged and vibrated against in his pocket. And again. And then again. He yanked it free and kicked his boots out of the way, glancing at the screen. This time it was Luca. Short and sweet. Not suggesting, but insisting he and Tessa both get their asses back to the villa. Now. A cold knot congealed in the pit of his stomach. Had something happened with Calli? "Later."

Chapter Sixteen

Alec materialized in the kitchen of his mother's villa expecting to find everyone gathered there. Instead, he found only his sister Callista, sipping a tall glass of blood orange juice, and devouring an enormous wedge of fruit *torta*.

"Hey, Cal, what's up?"

"My weight," she mumbled around a mouthful of pie. "If your niece doesn't make an appearance soon, Luca can rent me out as an airship."

"Nah, you're too heavy to get off the ground," he laughed, jumping back as she speared the fork in the direction of his midsection.

"Where's Tessa?"

"Upstairs. We brought some of her clothes back with us and she's putting them away. Where is everybody?" Based on Luca's cryptic text, Alec expected to arrive in the middle of a crisis.

"In the den. With Mother and someone called Galen. I gather he's a *Defensori* friend of Luca's." Callista picked up her glass and took a long draught of juice. "Your wife is lovely, Alec. You need to work it out."

"Done deal, I hope. Galen? Yeah, I know him. What's he doing here?"

"No idea." Callista broke off another piece of the crisp, fruit filled tart and brought the fork to her lips with a shrug. "No one tells me anything these days. Luca closed himself up in the den last night after you left, and then Galen arrived early this morning. Mother shoved a *torta* in my face, and then went to join them. 'Relax,' she said. 'Put your feet up,' she said. Of course, I haven't actually seen my feet in over a month. I wish people would stop treating me like the least little stress might kill me. I am not some fragile little flower."

"No, you aren't." Anyone who survived over a century of captivity with a madman, and then escaped from a sealed tomb in time to prevent a pissed off demon from attacking the man she loved could hardly be considered fragile. In fact, beneath his little sister's delicate appearance and generous heart lurked one of the strongest women he'd ever known. After mourning her loss for so long, his heart swelled every time he clapped eyes on her. Sometimes he still had trouble believing they'd actually gotten her back. "Eat your *torta* and enjoy the coddling while it lasts. You'll have your hands full soon enough."

"It will be a welcome change," she said between bites.

"Let's see if you still feel that way a few months from now." He laughed, dropping a kiss on top of her dark head and heading for the den.

Tessa bounded down the steps just as he reached the bottom. She snagged his belt loop in her fingers and tugged him to a halt in the doorway of the den when she spied the bald giant sporting dime-sized ear gauges with Japanese throwing stars, called shurikens, tattooed all over his shaved skull. Galen hunched over a laptop screen on the desk, his shoulders half as wide as the desk itself. He glanced up as they entered. He sat back, crossed his arms over his massive chest, and cocked a brow, eyes twinkling as the corners of his lips turned up.

"Wow." Tessa's voice echoed in his head. *"Who is he?"*

"No one you need to be ogling."

"I'm not ogling, but I'm not blind. He's actually rather attractive once you get past the big and scary. It's the smile, I think. Or maybe the eyes. The green is so shocking and intense against that lovely caramel skin."

"Why do women always say that?" Alec shook his head. The guy looked like any other hulking behemoth to him.

"Because it's true?" Tessa poked him in the back, then reached for his left hand, lacing her fingers through his.

"About time you showed up." Galen pushed back from the desk and rose to his feet, towering over everyone in the room. He moved around the furniture with unexpected grace, and held out a hand to Alec. "Haven't seen your ugly mug since you took that *animorti* knife to the ribs."

"Oh, you must mean the time Katrina tricked you, and Jacques Rapier snatched her right out from under your nose." Alec grinned back, slapping his palm against Galen's, and jerking his head toward Tessa who'd gasped at the mention of the injury.

"Yeah, well. Your sister-in-law is quite a persuasive witch when she sets her mind to something. And who knew her cousin would turn out to be a two-faced bitch? Anyway, that damn blade barely scratched you." Galen grinned, squeezing Alec's hand to let him know he'd gotten the message. "You didn't need to carry on like a little girl."

"Not exactly how I remember it." Alec grinned back, pulling Tessa forward. "Meet my wife. This is Contessa. Tess, this big, ugly brute with the selective memory is Galen. He's the *Defensori's* technology whiz kid."

"Contessa." Galen nodded.

"Just Tessa," she smiled back, squeezing Alec's fingers. "Hello, Galen."

"Galen also descends from the line of Menelik, better known as King David, son of Solomon and Makeda. Which makes him the *Defensori's* resident *Djinn* expert, too," Luca interjected, and Alec's mouth dropped open. "And before you ask, the stories are true. Makeda, Queen of Sheba, was a *Djinniyah*."

Alec picked up his jaw and expelled a long, low whistle between his teeth.

"Half, anyway. On her mother's side." Galen grunted, returning to his post behind the desk. "You know what they say. Can't pick your relatives."

"Well, I guess an ancestry including an Ethiopian queen explains the lovely caramel skin." Alec winked at Tessa. Galen lifted his gaze from the computer screen and arched a brow in Alec's direction.

"I'm flattered, Alec. But, you aren't my type, no matter how pretty you are."

"Very funny. And we need a *Djinn* expert, why?"

"Tessa," Alec's mother interrupted, reaching for Tessa's other hand and tugging her toward the door. "Why don't we go and see what Callista is up to? You must be hungry. I'll put a fresh pot of coffee on, and

I've got a lovely cherry *torta*."

"The way Calli was going at it, I'd guess the *torta's* been reduced to crumbs too small for mice by now," Alec laughed. "We've eaten. And Mom? I'm sorry about last night. I know you were only trying to help. And though you shouldn't interpret this in any way as free rein to meddle in my life in the future, thanks."

Tessa beamed and leaned in close to his side.

"Really, Alec. As though I could ever be *that* mother." His mother waved him off, but Alec caught the gleam of moisture in her eyes. "And you're welcome. Are you coming, Tessa?"

"Actually." Tessa glanced from the small notebook in Luca's hand, to the papers piled beside the laptop in front of Galen, and then finally looked up at Alec. "If this has something to do with my father, I'd really rather stay, if that's okay?"

"She'll have to know sooner or later," Luca sighed, waving the notebook in Madge's direction before tossing it on the desk. Alec's mother threw her hands in the air and made her escape. "May as well be sooner."

"Know what?" Tessa asked.

"How well did you look at this stuff yesterday?" Luca indicated the notebook and paperwork on the desk.

"My examination was cursory, at best," Alec responded. "To tell you the truth, last night I even considered the idea Barachiel left it as a red herring. Part of the whole plot to bring Tess and me together."

"Always a possibility, I suppose. But, I don't think so. Calli passed out early last night, and I found myself at loose ends, so I started reading through it. Barachiel had dealings with MFAA, as you suspected. The notebook contains a list of dates and places. Merkers, Altaussee, Seiger. Galen cross referenced the list and confirmed they represent known repositories of paintings, ceramics, books, and religious treasures plundered by the Nazis and the dates the Allies discovered and reclaimed them."

"Fairly common knowledge to anyone who's done any research on the topic, I imagine." Alec shrugged. He led Tessa over to one of the armchairs by the window, then perched a hip against it, draping an arm across the back once she settled into it. "Hitler was a frustrated artist who fancied himself an art connoisseur. The war provided the opportunity to pick and choose among the greatest European masterpieces and acquire them for himself and his cronies. He planned to turn the Austrian city of Linz into the cultural capital of the Third Reich with Führermuseum as the centerpiece."

"A plan never realized," Luca nodded. "The notebook also contains references to Breslau, which was transferred to Poland in the aftermath of the war and renamed Wrocław. Although it's never been proven, according to local legend, as the Soviets approached near the end of the war, a train or trains left Breslau laden with treasure and armaments the Nazis were determined to keep from the Allies. Supposedly, these trains were driven into a system of tunnels under the mountains that were part of an unfinished Nazi secret project near Wałbrzych, and buried."

"None of this is exactly classified information, Luca. Treasure hunters have been combing the mountains looking for those trains for years." Alec frowned.

"True. What's less commonly known, however, is how those tunnels are rumored to have been constructed. Galen, would you care to explain?"

Galen glanced up from the screen, punched at the keyboard, then leaned back in the chair and folded his arms over his chest. "*Djinn.*"

"Say what?" Alec's spine stiffened and an icy finger tickled the back of his neck. He glanced at Tessa from the corner of his eye and saw her posture straighten, as well. Luca's flip comment yesterday about the necklace resembling a *Djinn* trap echoed in his head. Suddenly, the childish sketch mixed in among Barachiel's papers appeared a lot less random.

"Hitler and other high ranking members of the Third Reich were fascinated with magic and the supernatural," Galen continued. "In fact, the Nazi organization itself started as an occult fraternity before it later morphed into a political party. Himmler established a paranormal research team as far back as nineteen thirty-five, and Hitler believed the possession of certain holy relics would give him paranormal powers, ensure his victory in the war, and show him the gateway to a higher metaphysical realm."

"Sounds like a bad movie plot," Alec muttered. "Well, we know he didn't win the war. So much for the supernatural powers. And this gateway, you think he found it?"

"Doubtful, but that doesn't mean he didn't find *something.*" Galen uncrossed his arms and sat forward, planting his palms on the cluttered surface of the desk. "What I do know is an Elder *Djinni* went missing toward the end of the Nazi tunnel construction in the Owl Mountains. Historically, we know the Nazis created at least seven underground structures, with construction carried out by forced laborers and prisoners. But, the physical abuse, malnutrition, and typhus would have weakened and significantly diminished the available and able-bodied work force. As the Allies approached, the Nazis would have become more and more desperate. None of the known structures were ever finished. Yet, at the end, with limited resources and while basically on the run, the Nazis somehow constructed something large enough to conceal one or more trains, and complex enough that it remains undiscovered over a half century later? Seems unlikely. But, consider if one of their sorcerers actually managed to conjure and capture a respected *Djinni* and hold his continued well-being over the heads of his kin in exchange for their labor..." Galen left the sentence dangling.

"Okay, suppose the Nazi did conjure and bind a *Djinni*. Why stop at building secret tunnels? Why not harness them to turn the tide of the war in the Germans' favor?" Alec pressed his lips together and started to cross his arms over his chest. Glancing down, he saw Tessa twisting her wedding band around and around her finger again. It was a habit he'd never noticed before, but one he'd come to recognize as a sure sign of discomfort. He slipped a hand beneath her hair and cupped the nape of her neck, rubbing the knots from her muscles with his thumb and forefinger. Still the twisting persisted.

"Maybe he managed to convince the Nazis he and his people didn't have that kind of power," Tessa whispered. "They had no stake in a human war."

"Why do you say that?" Alec frowned.

"I don't know." Tessa lifted wide, worried eyes to his. "The thought just popped into my head."

"Interesting." Luca arched a brown. "Tessa, what can you tell us about the necklace?"

"Nothing, really." Tessa turned her attention to Luca. "Only what I told Alec yesterday."

"Would you mind repeating it for our benefit?"

"Of course not." Tessa shrugged. She reached to lay a hand on Alec's thigh and he covered it with his. Alec watched the reaction of the two *Defensori* as she recounted the same story she shared with him the previous day. Luca's brows rose higher, while Galen's descended lower.

"Even if the necklace is a *Djinn* trap, simply touching it shouldn't produce such an extreme reaction," Galen said, shaking his head, his brows still drawn together.

"True," Luca agreed. "Unless, of course, the person touching it is exquisitely psychometric. Like Tessa."

Chapter Seventeen

"Hell, yeah, that could make a difference." Galen's lips twisted in a grimace and he glared at Luca. "It didn't occur to you to mention that a little sooner?"

"I had no idea it had any bearing on the situation until now." Luca shrugged and levered his big body away from the bookcase. Crossing the room, he propped a hip on the corner of the desk.

"I don't understand." Tessa squeezed Alec's hand as Galen rose to his feet and came to stand in front of her. She looked up. Way up. He'd reverted to big and scary. At least the scowl softened as he looked away from Luca and turned his attention to her.

"Think hard, Tessa. When you came in contact with the necklace, did you touch the stone itself, or only the metal cage?" Galen asked, regarding her intently.

"I have no idea. As I told Alec yesterday, I remember very little of what happened once I touched it."

"I may be able to access what you can't. Assuming you actually came into physical contact with a *Djinni,* my ancestry should give me the ability to trace the path of those memories. If you're willing to let me try?" He directed the question to Alec, who stiffened beside her and shifted closer. "You have my word I'll respect your privacy and seek out only those specific memories."

"I…what do you think?" Tessa turned to Alec. His

lips compressed to a thin line as he looked first at Luca, and then at Galen.

"Is it dangerous?" he asked.

"Dangerous? Doubtful. Memories can't do physical harm. But," Galen locked gazes with Tessa, "it could be...unpleasant. When people repress things, it's usually for good reason. It's the mind's way of protecting itself. If I start poking around, it may trigger memories you'd rather leave buried."

"I don't like it," Alec snapped. "If you've already decided the necklace is a *Djinn* trap, then fine. I'm happy to take your word for it. Mystery solved. What will tormenting my wife tell you?"

"Perhaps nothing. Perhaps everything," Luca said slowly. "Like you, I assumed Barachiel's MFAA references indicated perhaps he'd found clues to an as yet undiscovered cache of plunder. Important, but not urgent. However, taken together with the information in the notebook and his deliberate inclusion of the drawing, I suspect he's been tracking this *Djinni* for years, and he intended for you to finish the job and find it."

"You said it yourself, Luca. *Djinn* aren't enamored with humans, and even good *Djinn* have their own agenda and shouldn't be trusted. Why should I concern myself with finding one that's been taken out of circulation?" Tessa never knew Alec to back down from a challenge, from diving head first into a riddle. Warmth filled her heart as she realized his hesitation to pursue this one stemmed from concern for her.

"If the *Djinni* in that trap is the missing Elder, as I believe it is, I know him. No, he's not especially fond of humans, but neither did he have any particular grievance against them. He was content to exist in his own realm. Trust me, he *did* have the power to influence the outcome of the war if he was so inclined," Galen responded. "I think it says something about his character that he didn't. Even when it might have gained him liberty."

"Someone conjured and captured him against his will," Tessa said. "He deserves his freedom. You know it's the right thing to do. Memories can't hurt me, Alec."

"The right thing means shit to me if it hurts you." His response echoed in her head.

Tessa tugged his hand to her lips and pressed them to his knuckles.

"You won't let it hurt me."

Alec looked at her for a long moment, then shot to his feet. Dragging her out of the chair, he dropped into it, and then pulled her sideways across his lap, locking his arms around her.

"Well, if he didn't have a quarrel with humans before, don't you think he might have a damn good reason to pick a fight now?" Alec grumbled.

"Maybe, but *Djinn* generally direct their vengeance at those who caused the insult. Besides, there's another concern. Madge tells me *animorti* showed up at the flat where Barachiel's things are stored. It seems likely someone suspected what he'd stumbled on to and saw his death as an opportunity to see what he'd found. As you know, *Fallen* infiltrated the highest ranks of the Nazi party. They lost the battle, but that doesn't mean they've given up the war. A *Djinni* who might know the location of the remaining lost gold and has the power to help them give rise to the Fourth Reich would be quite a prize."

"Shit," Alec muttered.

"Succinct, but apt," Luca drawled.

"And what do you expect to garner from Tessa's memories?"

"Maybe nothing," Galen answered. "But, even bound, the *Djinni* would have awareness of everything going on around him. If Tessa touched the stone confining him, and if the *Djinni* sensed her psychometric abilities, it's possible he transferred some of those perceptions to her. If so, it could be incredibly helpful."

"*If* she touched it? *If* he sensed it? *If* it's the *Djinni* you think it is? That's an awful lot of *ifs* to justify poking around in my wife's head, Galen."

"I'm aware of that." Galen regarded Alec steadily.

"I'm ready, Galen." She sat up straighter in Alec's lap. "What do you need me to do?"

"Now, wait just a minute—" Alec sputtered. He didn't like this idea. *At all.* He always protected her from his work, from the ugly side of anything, really.

"They're my memories. They can't hurt me, not really. And I want to help. I'm not a little girl anymore. This is my decision."

"I just—"

"Don't want me involved in this. I know." She laid a hand on his cheek and stroked the tense line of his jaw. *"But, I'm pretty sure I already am. Will it make you feel better if you accompany Galen?"*

"Well, I guess it won't make me feel worse." He nuzzled his face into her palm and pressed his lips to the center, his breath hot and moist against her skin. Then he sighed, straightened, and shifted her weight in

his lap.

"Okay, let's do this. But, I'll be right there. If there's any risk to her at all, you get the hell out. Got it?"

"Understood." Galen bobbed his head, and lowered himself into the other chair. Luca moved to the desk and took the seat behind it. Cranking the top off of a bottle of water sitting on the corner, he took a long swig before propping his elbows on the top, and lacing his fingers under his chin.

"What do I do?" Tessa asked.

"You just relax and drop every shield you're conscious of. Alec, you lock onto me and stay close."

Tessa closed her eyes and let her head fall back against Alec's shoulder. She felt his nod as he rested his cheek on the top of her head. Tessa licked lips gone dry. What if the memories she'd repressed really did turn out to be something she'd rather leave buried? Was she crazy to agree to this? Then she thought of her father. He considered this important enough to leave the evidence for Alec to decipher. She thought of the *Djinni*, conjured and captured against his will. Galen thought he'd tried reaching out to her for help. Didn't she owe it to both of them to swallow her own misgivings and at least try? Of course, she did. She burrowed into Alec's chest and dropped every shield she'd consciously put in place. Whatever happened, he would keep her safe.

"I'm ready," she whispered. Galen answered by tentatively touching her mind. Alec zoomed in and locked onto him. She squirmed in Alec's arms as the two *Earthbound* fought for dominance. They'd barely begun and a dull ache already bloomed behind her eyes.

Maybe this had been a mistake, after all. This wasn't supposed to be painful. Not physically, at least.

"This isn't going to work if you fight me, Alec."

Her discomfort eased the moment she felt Alec back off and allow Galen to take the lead. This must be what people meant when they referred to their lives flashing before their eyes. Like the flickering glare of an old projector in a dark theater, people and places twinkled and faded. Her father's laughing eyes, her mother's cool hand stroking her fevered brow, that magical moment when she'd first met Alec. So many things unconsciously stored away, now recalled with the sharp focus of a well-honed blade. All of it rushing by, begging to be grasped, yet refusing to pause and be captured. Galen continued to dig, beyond recollection, beneath the darkness, until they all found themselves smothering in her nightmares. Scenes and sounds broke apart, each piece a jagged mirror reflecting a new horror. Galen's shock and Alec's confusion strained the edges of her awareness. Her mind screamed at her to wake up. But, she couldn't. Because she wasn't asleep. And she recognized it now. Recognized *him*. Never a dream, not a nightmare, but a presence. A raw scream tore from her throat, and she arched against Alec fighting to free herself. Blinding pain shredded all rational thought as Alec ripped Galen free of the blackness, dragging her along with them. The threat trailed her, a shadowy hand grasping through the murky haze of her sanity. Thankfully, before the approaching madness claimed her, blessed oblivion descended.

Alec panted as his full consciousness slammed back into his head. *What in the hell was that?* He frantically repositioned Tessa's limp body in his arms.

Panic clawed its way up his throat and pounded against the inside of his skull as he regarded his wife's deathly stillness. He pawed clumsily at the smooth column of her throat, unable to breathe until he felt the slow, but steady thrum against his shaking fingertips. Yeah, she was alive, but what if they'd damaged her mind?

Alec glanced up as Galen dropped to the floor at his feet and reached toward Tessa.

"Let me—"

"Don't. Touch. Her." Alec hissed through clenched teeth, gathering her more closely against his chest. He'd been a fool to allow this. Discussing his work with her, listening to her feedback, walking away from it at the end of the day, putting her first? Priorities, setting limits, those things he could do. Those things he *would* do. But, risking Tessa for answers? No more. Not happening again. "You told her—us—she would be safe. She trusted you."

"I didn't expect—"

"I don't give a rat's ass what you expected. What in the hell happened?"

Tessa stirred and her eyes fluttered open, a deep, shocking blue against the pallor of her skin. They darted around wildly, then filled with a look of relief as they focused on Alec's face above her.

"Hey," she croaked, her lips curving into a wan smile. "You don't look so good."

"You've had better moments, yourself," he smiled back, smoothing her hair from her face, his hand lingering to cup her cheek. Good thing he had no reason to stand. Who knew relief could turn a guy's bones to rubber? "You scared the shit out of me."

"I'm okay." She cleared her throat, wincing as she

attempted to push up to a sitting position. "I think."

Luca appeared next to the chair. Alec snagged the open bottle of water being waved under his nose and brought it to Tessa's lips. She covered his hand with one of her own, tipped the bottle, and sucked at it greedily until not a drop remained. Then she fell against his chest and turned her head toward Galen.

"The *Djinni* transferred a little more than his perceptions when I touched the stone, didn't he?"

"I knew *Djinn* could possess humans, but this?" Galen shook his head, his green eyes wide. "You aren't human, and it's not possession. Exactly. I'm not even sure it's possible."

"Well, clearly it's possible," Tessa returned dryly. She struggled to sit up. Alec hauled her upright, relieved her color was returning, but kept her locked within the circle of his arms. "We've just seen it. And I'm half human."

Luca stepped back and dropped into the chair Galen vacated.

"Would one of you care to explain what the hell you're babbling about?" Alec grumbled.

"Now, I don't want you to get upset," Tessa turned in his arms and patted his cheek. Cajoling him? A prickle of unease skittered down his spine. The intensity increased as she dropped her hand, glanced at Galen, and commenced twisting her ring. The giant remained cross-legged on the floor, staring down at the pattern of the tile, and avoiding Alec's gaze. "After all, it was an accident. Right, Galen?"

Galen's massive chest expanded as he sucked in a deep breath. He held it a moment, then blew it out through flaring nostrils and rose to his feet in one fluid, graceful motion. He glanced over at Luca, who stiffened and sat forward gripping the arms of the chair, ramping up Alec's sense of foreboding. Finally, he rolled his shoulders and smiled briefly at Tessa before locking his gaze on Alec.

"Yeah, it was an accident."

"What was?"

"When Tessa touched the stone, the *Djinni* sensed her gift and tried to reach out for help. Unfortunately, unfamiliar with psychometricians, he miscalculated. More than his memories and perceptions crossed over into her mind. Part of his actual consciousness is trapped there."

Chapter Eighteen

"Well, tell him to get the hell out," Alec roared, once he regained the power of speech. Tessa's gasp alerted him to his crushing grip, and he immediately loosened his arms. She climbed from his lap, heading for the small fridge under the bookshelf. She grabbed another bottle of water, and raised it to her lips with shaking hands.

"It isn't quite that simple." Galen shook his head, rubbing the back of his neck. "Tessa's nightmares? His attempts to gain her attention when her mind rested. Over the years, they've become worse? Darker? More frequent?"

"Yes." Tessa polished off another bottle of water and returned to perch on the arm of Alec's chair. Her fingers burrowed into the hair at his nape, kneading the tense knots in the muscles of his neck.

"Like us, *Djinn* live for centuries, but they aren't immortal. This situation is unprecedented, and from what I gathered before you yanked me out, the longer he exists in this divided state, the weaker he becomes. If he isn't able to reunite his two halves, eventually he'll cease to exist. He's desperate. Flexing his muscles, so to speak. Trying to become the dominant consciousness to ensure his survival."

"At the expense of Tessa's." Her fingers on his neck stilled.

"He isn't malicious, Alec. It's self-preservation."

"Yeah, well my wife isn't going to be sacrificed to save his ass." He shot to his feet and stalked across the room to the desk, scooping up the notebook and flipping it open. "That's what this is all about. Barachiel knew. We find the necklace, free the *Djinni*, and he abandons his little domicile in Tessa's head to make nice with his other half. Right?"

"It seems a reasonable assumption." Luca offered his first contribution to the conversation. "Even though he relinquished his immortality, Barachiel retained his psychometric and telepathic powers. There's no doubt he would have explored Tessa's memories after learning of her reaction to the necklace."

"And never tell me?"

"I expect he thought he was protecting you. He'd locate the *Djinn* trap eventually and rectify the situation. Did he know your nightmares had worsened?" Tessa shook her head, and Luca continued. "Therefore, he didn't realize the status quo changed, didn't recognize the stakes were higher. There was no particular urgency. He left the information for Alec, secure in the knowledge he'd ferret out the truth sooner or later."

"And I will." Alec glanced up from the notebook to see Tessa, still perched on the arm of the chair nervously twisting her ring. Every puzzle he ever pieced together became meaningless beside this one. His bright, beautiful Tessa. He wasn't about to allow some frustrated freaking *Djinni* to steal her sanity. Her keen intelligence, sharp wit, and musical genius belonged to her. And she belonged to him.

"Sooner, not later. I swear to you."

"So, what do we know so far?" Alec mused aloud. "The Nazis conjure a *Djinni*. When he refuses to turn the tide of the war in their favor, they trap him in the necklace and hold his well-being over the heads of his clansmen to ensure their cooperation in completing tunnels to house their plunder and keep it out of the hands of the Allies. Somehow, this mystery woman discovers the truth about the necklace, and steals it. Then attempts to deliver it to Barachiel. Why?"

"She's not a mystery woman," Galen said. "I saw her in Tessa's memories. Her name was Gerta Beringer, and she worked as a curator at the Kaiser Friedrich Museum in Berlin before the war. Well-known and highly respected in the art world, she traveled extensively, and dealt with every major museum in Europe."

"That explains how she knew my father. Though it doesn't explain how she acquired the *Djinni* in the first place, or why she thought my father, a simple art historian known to her as Eduardo Bartolucci, would have any idea what to do with it," Tessa pointed out.

"Whether she knew about either the *Djinni* or your father's true identity, his work to save artistic and cultural treasures would have been common knowledge in those circles." Galen said. "Who wouldn't perceive an ornate piece of jewelry with a stone that size, and in Nazi possession, as something significant that had most likely been stolen and should probably be saved? As to how she acquired it, it just so happens Gerta was also the younger sister of a very well-placed Nazi official."

"You knew her?" Tessa asked.

"Casually. We crossed paths in France a time or two working with the Resistance." Galen nodded.

"Rabidly anti-Nazi, she spent most of the war working against them in whatever way she could. Rumor had it she even wrote letters demanding the release of certain prisoners to commandants of the camps, signing only her surname. This, of course, fostered the impression the letters were from her much feared older brother. I imagine her actions saved more than one hapless victim. Beringer must have suspected her activities, but despite their different philosophies, he apparently chose to look the other way."

"So, your hypothesis is that her brother had the necklace in his possession and she somehow snatched it out from under his nose and secreted it to Italy?" Luca asked.

"It seems the most reasonable explanation." Galen shrugged. "Her connections allowed her to travel with few questions, and she would have wanted to get it as far away as possible before anyone noticed it missing. Though according to the *Djinni's* memories, she believed she was followed when she traveled to Italy."

"You think her brother finally turned on her?" Alec looked up from the notebook.

"Maybe. If he'd been entrusted with the *Djinni* and lost it, my guess is his ass would be in a sling. Of course, let's not forget about the *Fallen*. There were plenty of them in the inner circle, who would certainly have been interested, as well."

"How the necklace may have gotten into Tessa's hands in the first place is all interesting speculation," Luca observed, rising to his feet and stretching his arms over his head until his spine cracked. Then he moved toward the door. "But, it's probably more productive to concentrate on the more pressing concern. Where is it now?"

"Where do you two think you're going?" Alec snapped, as Galen made a move to follow Luca.

"I'm going to check on my wife, and Galen has an appointment with our fearless leader. It appears in his lengthy absence, Galen's ancestral home has been overrun by squatters who have a certain reluctance to leave." Luca bit back a smile. "You're the Riddle King, Alec. Figure it out. When you do, we'll go get it. We've got your back. You know that."

"Yeah, but…" He raked a hand through his hair. Sure, he might be the one known for figuring out the puzzle, and he knew Luca and Galen, or any of the *Defensori* for that matter, would back him up. But, for a man who'd always preferred to work alone, now he found himself open to all the help he could get. Because this wasn't some magical ring or a demon binding grimoire. This wasn't one of Michael's ill-conceived gifts to his progeny. Failure could cost Tessa her mind and quite possibly her life if this *Djinni* became desperate. He'd lost her once through his own blind indifference. He wasn't about to lose her again.

"Yeah, I'll let you know if I come up with anything." He sighed and dropped into the chair as the door closed behind them, and pulled the notebook in front of him, his eyes skimming the elegant script, brain cells struggling to make sense of it. He'd figure it out. He had no other option. He glanced up in surprise as Tessa's long, delicate fingers splayed across the pages of the notebook.

"May I?"

"Be my guest." Alec pushed the book across the desk to Tessa. "I had a thought we should start by trying to find this Angelina you suspected of having made off with the necklace. But, based on your father's early entries, it appears great minds think alike. It was one of the first things he did. According to his notes, he found her sister. Angelina traded the necklace to a Nazi official in exchange for safe passage to Switzerland for herself and her family. The family made it, but along the way, she disappeared. My assumption would be the Nazi feared she knew more than she let on and double crossed her. No big surprise there. After that, your father documents extensive travels through Eastern Europe. The most recent entries are written in some kind of code. I hate to waste the time, but I may have to hightail it over to my flat in Paris and grab a couple of reference books to figure it out."

Tessa's eyes narrowed and her forehead pleated into deep furrows as she flipped through the pages, running a forefinger from right to left, top to bottom, like the star pupil of a speed reading course. Alec watched her, barely daring to breathe. Would her gift kick in and pick up some errant memory of her father's to explain the odd combination of letters scribbled across the final pages? Hey, a guy could hope.

"He's been looking almost my entire life," Tessa murmured. "Why did he never tell me? Or you? Or anyone, for that matter? Michael, you, the *Defensori*...surely someone would have been able to help. All those trips, all those countries...I thought we travelled so much because of his business. And we did. Just not the art business. He searched right up until it must have become physically impossible for him to do so. These last entries are dated just a few months ago."

"Yep. And they're the ones he entered in code. I

assume he found something and wanted to ensure the *Fallen* wouldn't be able to access it if something happened before he could get it to us. As to why he never told anyone or asked for help, I can only guess. Knowing him as I did, I suspect he blamed himself for leaving you alone and vulnerable. He felt he, alone, had to rectify it."

"That's ridiculous. He did important work, and he didn't leave me alone. Hundreds of people surrounded me. It wasn't his fault."

"I agree. But, it's no more ridiculous than my brother blaming himself for our sister's abduction. In the end, with Kat's life at stake, he finally realized people make their own decisions."

"Kat?"

"Katrina, his wife. Sorry, forgot you haven't met her yet. She's a peach."

"I'm sure. So you were saying your brother finally asked for help?"

"Not asked, so much as allowed," Alec laughed. "You know Kass. Letting Luca and the other *Defensori* assist was fine. But, he sure as hell wasn't happy when my bleeding carcass crossed his threshold. It was hardly a scratch, but you would have sworn I'd been decapitated."

"He didn't want to lose you, too."

"I get that, but taking care of me isn't his job, and he needed to realize it. Anyway, it was a one-time deal. My mother doesn't need two sons putting their lives on the line on an almost daily basis to keep her up at night." Alec shifted in the chair and shrugged. "My point is, he didn't allow anyone to share the burden until he ran out of options, just like your father. Now, about this code. It makes things a bit more challenging, but I'll figure it out. I swear to you, Tess. I'll head over to Paris tonight, get the code books, and hustle back here and crack it. Then I'll figure out where the necklace is and get that damn *Djinni* out of your head and out of our lives."

"I know you will." Tessa's lips curled upward as she flipped the notebook closed and handed it to him across the desk. "But, you won't need to go to Paris. We only have to go to the *Borgo*."

"You saw something? A vision?" Alec's heart kicked him in the ribs as he shot to his feet and snatched the notebook from her hand. "Do you know where it is?"

"Not exactly. But, I do recognize the code. I guess my father really was determined we should do this together, because I'm probably the only one who would, considering he and I made it up. It's not an actual code. It's a game. My father invented it to encourage me to practice as a child. The letters transpose into music. We don't need a code book. We need a piano."

Chapter Nineteen

"Chopin," Tessa announced as her fingers stilled on the keys and the final strains of the music echoed off of the walls and faded. She closed the notebook and spun on the piano stool to face Alec. "It's the third movement from Chopin's Piano Sonata number two. The Funeral March."

"Funeral March, huh? So something to do with his death? Didn't he die in France?" Alec asked, turning to Galen, whom he'd asked to meet them at the *Borgo* flat following his meeting with Michael. "You said you'd met this Gerta Beringer in France a time or two."

"Yes. He died in Paris." Tessa closed the lid over the keys and rose to her feet. "But, he was born in Poland. And that's where his heart remains. Literally, not just figuratively. At his request, upon his death, Chopin's body was opened and his heart removed. His body lies in Père Lachaise Cemetery, but his heart was returned to Poland. You know my father. Always the first one to follow his heart. Maybe that's what he's telling us to do."

"Follow the heart? So we're back to Poland. The hidden tunnels and lost Nazi treasure?" Alec asked.

"Maybe," Galen responded, frowning at his laptop screen as his fingers flew over the keys with a surprising speed and agility for a man with hands the size of dinner plates. "Looks like Chopin's heart took a wild ride. After his death, the organ was removed, as Tessa says, and sealed into a crystal jar filled with liquid, most often assumed to be cognac. Then it was placed in a mahogany urn and smuggled back into Poland, through the border guards, by his older sister, Ludwika. It bounced around between various relatives until 1879, when it was finally entombed in a church pillar in Warsaw."

"Where your treasure is, there your heart will be also," Tessa whispered, and Alec turned back to her.

"What?"

"The inscription on the pillar where Chopin's heart is interred. It's from the book of Matthew. Though his exile was self-imposed, his heart remained bound to his home. Like my father, I guess. He gave up everything for my mother and me. Exiled himself. In the end, part of him was happy to be returning home, at last."

"He never regretted his choice, you know. I'm surprised he told you." Though Barachiel confided as much to Alec, he wouldn't have expected him to be so frank with Tess.

"He didn't. But, I knew just the same. Knowing he's happy and free makes letting him go hurt just a little less, actually."

Alec reached out and folded her into his arms, pressing his lips to the top of her head. He was all over anything that made her father's absence easier for her to bear.

"Well, now we're getting somewhere," Galen said, glancing up from the screen with a wide smile splitting his face. "It seems after the heart was interred in Holy Cross church, it became an object of public veneration. People regarded it with a fervor usually reserved for the relics of saints. Since the tsarist authorities refused to permit any other public memorial to their native son, Chopin's heart, which he insisted return home, became a symbol of nationalism. By the time Poland gained independence in 1918, the thing became an outright shrine."

"But, that was before the Germans even entered the picture," Alec countered. "Where's the connection to the Nazis?"

"For a guy who's spent years carrying out methodical, meticulous research, you have the patience of a gnat, McAllister. Fast forward to the Warsaw Uprising of 1944. The Germans, well aware of Chopin's symbolic power, outlawed performances of his music. They exhumed the heart and stored it at the headquarters of the German commander of the regional forces for the remainder of the uprising."

"So, ironically, they had no problem systematically slaughtering the Poles who rebelled against them, but they protected the object they rallied around?" Alec shook his head.

"Don't forget, though they were conscious of the danger Chopin represented in uniting the Poles, the Nazis also believed he'd been influenced by German composers."

"So, he must have some redeeming qualities, right?"

"Something like that," Galen grinned. "Anyway, after they suppressed the uprising, the Germans made a big show of returning the heart to the Poles. Set up a film crew to record the transfer of the urn to the archbishop, and everything."

"No doubt an attempt to make themselves look

good," Tessa grumbled. "Propaganda was the Nazis' middle name."

"True," Galen agreed. "But, it didn't work out that way. Just as the transfer was about to take place, the lights malfunctioned, and the Nazis' plans for making a spectacle of the event and putting a positive spin on themselves, were ruined."

"This is all very interesting, but I still don't get how any of this ties in to the necklace," Alec said.

"Well, we know the woman who took the necklace, after Tessa dropped it, traded it to the Nazis, right? So, they got it back. Clearly, Barachiel is pointing us in the direction of Poland and Chopin's heart."

"I agree, I just don't see the connection."

"Well, consider this. After the urn was returned to the Poles, it didn't just get reinterred in the church pillar in Warsaw. The priests, fearing the Nazis would change their minds and demand it back, smuggled it outside of the city and hid it at St. Hedwig's in Milanówek. Rumor has it, once there, they decided to open the urn and make sure the Nazis hadn't stolen the heart and returned an empty container. Maybe the heart's not the only thing they found inside."

"So, if a member of the Nazi command in Warsaw somehow came into possession of the necklace, whether he knew it was a *Djinn* trap or not, he'd suspect it had value based on the size of the stone alone. What better place to hide something valuable until the war ended and he could reclaim it than an urn which would be re-interred?" Alec widened his eyes as his intellect finally superseded his concern, and kicked in. Luca called him the Riddle King, but from the moment the threat to Tessa became apparent, his ability to reason logically left the building.

"Exactly. I did a little digging on Beringer, too. Since he moved in the upper ranks, there's quite a bit of biographical information to be found. Guess who turns up as part of the command structure in Poland at the time of the Warsaw Uprising?"

"That has to be it!" Alex said. "Gerta steals the necklace, smuggles it to Italy, and her brother catches on and follows. He tails her to the *Palazzo Pitti*, waits, watches, and sees Angelina scoff it up in the chaos of Tessa's reaction. He gets her alone, tricks her into trading it for passage, and when she thinks she's safe, ensures she can never identify him. Later, he's assigned to Warsaw, and with the war crashing down around the Reich, he starts looking ahead. What happened to Gerta?"

"No clue. Can't find any record of her after the war," Galen said, tapping on the keys and squinting at the monitor. "One thing's for sure, if Beringer did conceal the necklace in the urn, it must have been removed and hidden elsewhere before the heart was returned to Warsaw in '45. The authorities opened that pillar again in 2014 amidst concerns the jar may have been damaged, allowing the heart to deteriorate. They kept the findings pretty hush-hush, but according to the limited press releases, the heart was fine, and there was no indication anything unusual had been found in there with it."

"If he went to the trouble of following his sister all the way to Italy to get his hands on the necklace, wouldn't he have attempted to retrieve it from its hiding place after the war?" Tessa asked.

"Well, we don't know that he didn't," Galen said

absently as he continued to click and scroll through the information on the screen. "But, I think it's unlikely. The prevailing theory is Beringer and his family used the ratlines to escape to South America right before the fall of Berlin. I'd bet he was far more concerned with survival and evading the Nazi hunters than retrieval at that point."

"Ratlines?"

"Ratlines were a complex system of escape routes for Nazis and other fascists fleeing Europe at the end of the war. They mainly led toward havens in South America. In fact, there are still many who believe Hitler didn't die in his Berlin bunker, but instead traveled a ratline through Spain, and lived out his remaining years in hiding in an isolated location in Argentina."

"So, if we assume Beringer had access to the urn, and then hid the necklace in it, and we also assume it wouldn't have been worth the risk for him to try to return and reclaim it, all roads lead to the church in Milanówek?" Alec asked.

Galen nodded, snapped the laptop closed, and rose to his feet. "I know it seems like a lot of supposition, but based on the clues Barachiel left, combined with what we've discovered today, that's the direction I'm leaning."

"I owe you, Galen." Alec stuck out a hand. "I know I'm usually the puzzle guy, but in this case, I was spinning my wheels in a swamp. You make a damn fine researcher."

"Hell, you don't owe me a thing. You would have figured it out eventually. You're just too close to this one to think straight. Happens when your heart's involved."

"Well, eventually isn't good enough in this case, so I *do* owe you. Thanks."

"No problem." Galen bobbed his head slightly. "So, when do we leave?"

"Yes, when do we leave?" Tessa piped up, tugging on Alec's shirt like an anxious child.

"*We* don't," Alec responded. "*You* will stay right here where you're safe. With Calli so close to term, I would never ask Luca to leave her side, so he'll be here for protection in the event of trouble. And Galen, much as I appreciate the offer, you have your own issues to deal with at the moment. You've already helped enormously."

"Not how it works, Alec." Galen folded his arms over his chest. "You said it yourself. Luca isn't leaving Callista. And Mac is busy finishing up the deal in New York. I have nothing going on that can't wait. I know more about *Djinn* than anyone in our immediate circle. I've seen you fight, and while I know you're as capable as any *Defensori*, no one goes in alone. No one. I'm coming with you. Deal with it."

Before Alec could open his mouth in response, Tessa stepped out of his embrace and crossed her arms over her chest, mimicking Galen's posture.

"Ditto."

Alec found himself hard pressed not to burst out laughing at the determination in her delicate features.

"Ditto? That's the best you've got?"

"Of course not." She pushed out her lower lip and widened her stance. "Just the most expedient and succinct. I'm coming with you. Deal with it."

"No, you aren't, so *you* deal with it."

"Alec, be reasonable." Tessa dropped her arms to

her sides and sighed. "If you and Galen are right and you manage to find the necklace, is it really the best course of action to traipse halfway across the continent, possibly dodging the *Fallen*, to bring it back here? Surely it makes more sense for me to be right there, so the *Djinni* can be freed and immediately reunited with the consciousness currently making itself at home in my head. Besides, my gift might come in handy. I could help. Don't you agree, Galen?"

Alec fixed a warning glare on the larger man.

"Uh-uh." The giant glared right back, then his expression softened as he switched his attention to Tessa and shook his head. "Sorry, Tess, but when it comes to getting between mates, I am neutral. Just call me Switzerland."

"But, you agree with her, don't you?" Alec pressed his lips together and sent the mental message.

"Let's say I understand your reluctance, but she makes a good point. Several, in fact."

"I know you don't like the idea." Tessa moved in front of Alec and laid her hands on his chest. "But, it doesn't change the fact I'm right. You know what they say. If you always do what you've always done, you'll always get what you've always had."

"Meaning I shut you out before and we ended up on opposite sides of the world?"

She leaned into him, and his arms came around her, enjoying the weight of her body pressed to his. He felt her nod against his chest.

"That, and I never pushed hard enough to *make* you include me. afraid if I pushed too hard, I'd push you away entirely. Neither of those approaches worked very well for us in the past, did they?" She tilted back her head, propped her chin on his chest, and smiled into his eyes. "So, I'm changing my strategy. Consider yourself pushed."

"Push all you want." Alec ground his teeth together and shook his head. He would not put her at risk no matter how sweetly she smiled, or how innocently she batted those big, blue eyes. "In this case, I'm not budging. Aside from the *Djinni*, we don't know who or what else we may be dealing with. Galen and I will go and track down the necklace, you will wait here. End of story."

"Then I guess we must be reading two completely different books, because that isn't how I see the end of the story, at all." She stepped back, pressed her lips together, and crossed her arms over her chest. "And just for the record, you sounded exactly like your brother, just then."

"I'll take that as a compliment. Thank you."

"I didn't intend it as one, but, hey, whatever floats your boat. You do remember I've been taking care of myself for ten years and lived to tell, right?"

"Yeah, well." Alec shifted from one foot to the other and looked away. "I didn't know you were alone and unprotected all that time."

"And what, exactly, would you have done if you'd known? Put your pride aside and come to apply for the job? I don't think so, Alec. Neither of us were ready. I'm not an idiot, and I have a very healthy sense of self-preservation."

"I don't doubt it, but having you with me will just give me one more thing to worry about."

"So, you're saying I'd be a distraction?"

"Worrying about your safety would be a

distraction," Alec replied, while acknowledging to himself the sight of Tessa sinking her even white teeth into her full lower lip already succeeded in distracting him for a moment. Still, he knew that look. She wouldn't take no for an answer, and no way in hell did he intend to bring her along. "However," he continued slowly as an idea occurred to him. "I guess it's true you actually could turn out to be helpful. Your gift might furnish us with information we might not otherwise be privy to."

"Really?" Tessa and Galen exclaimed in unison. Tessa's expression brightened, while the giant warrior's brow pleated.

"Yes, really." Alec drew her into his arms for a brief hug, then pressed his lips to her forehead, and pushed her in the direction of the door. "Now go have a cup of tea with my mother and Calli while Galen and I work out the logistics."

Chapter Twenty

"Yes, the stories are true. After the Nazis returned the urn containing the heart of Chopin to Holy Cross Church, the priests took no chances. They smuggled the urn here, to Milanówek, for safekeeping until the war ended." The young priest smiled across the desk at Alec and Galen. "A stroke of luck considering Holy Cross was nearly leveled during the conflict."

"The stories also say the priests opened the urn while it was here. Care to tell us what they found?" Alec asked, his intent stare registering the fleeting look of alarm flickering across the other man's features before he carefully schooled them into his former placid expression.

"They found the heart in a crystal jar of cognac, just as one would expect. Nothing more." Father Szczcuski averted his gaze, pushed back from the desk, and rose to his feet. "Now, if you'll excuse me, I have business to attend to in the sacristy."

A bolt of absolute rage brought Alec to his feet as he withdrew from the priest's mind, having read exactly what that business entailed. Galen sighed, rubbed a hand over his smooth pate, and shot to his feet beside him, planting a hand on Alec's chest when he would have lunged across the desk.

"You're lying, *Father*." Alec growled. "The priests *did* find something while the urn was here in

Milanówek. While you have no idea exactly what it is, you *do* know it's something of great value that whomever you're working for wants to keep hidden very badly. The fact you're willing to betray your vows and your office to maintain the secret...well, I guess that's between you and your maker. The fact you bound and gagged my wife in the sacristy? Now, that's between you and me, you sonofabitch."

"How...how did you know that?"

"I did warn you she'd be pissed that we left her behind. Granted, I never thought she'd be ticked enough to venture here on her own, but it's not like a couple of ropes and a lock can hold her..." Galen trailed off as Alec leveled a withering gaze in his direction.

"Not. The. Point. Can you find out everything he knows then wipe his memory so he has no recollection of any of us? I'm afraid if I do it in my current state of mind I may give him total and permanent amnesia." Galen nodded his assent. "Okay, after that, make sure the bastard can't bother us for a while and meet me in the church." All color drained from Szczcuski's face as he scurried around the far side of the desk. Galen faded and reappeared in front of the office door, crossed his arms over his massive chest, and blocked the priest's attempted escape.

"You don't understand," the priest sputtered, skidding to a halt, eyes widened. He held out his hands, palms up, as though in supplication. "They threatened my family...they keep them under constant surveillance...my parents, my sisters, the children. I care nothing for their secret. I want only to keep those I love safe from the threats."

"We're aware of that," Galen said. "Hence, the reason you're still breathing. Now, please go back to your desk and have a seat. You're going to take a little nap and when you wake up, you won't remember anything that happened today beyond what you ate for breakfast."

"How is that possible?" The priest shuffled backwards in the direction of the desk.

"You don't need to know. Please have a seat, Father." Alec waved a hand in the direction of the chair.

"They'll kill them. They'll kill me," the priest whimpered as he sank into the plush leather.

"Not if we kill them first," Galen muttered as Alec dematerialized and headed for the church.

****

"What in the hell do you think you're doing here?"

Tessa jumped, her palms flat against the back of the wooden vestment cabinet, as her heart lurched and slammed against the inside of her chest. Though he spoke softly, she didn't need her telepathic abilities, nor the unique connection of bound mates, to perceive Alec's rage. She straightened her spine, dropped her hands to her sides, and turned slowly to face him, surprised to find the air undisturbed by the anger rolling off of him in waves.

"Isn't it obvious? You said I could be helpful." Tessa swallowed hard and tried to shrug casually, wondering when her husband developed that odd little tic near the outer corner of his eye. "I'm helping. What took you so long?"

"We made a pit-stop. I thought when I left you behind a woman of your intelligence would figure out I didn't want you here and take the hint."

"You told me I could help, patted me on the head, and sent me off to tea. Then you left without me, and without another word." Tessa clenched her jaw until it ached, and blinked back the tears. "So, if you weren't trying to show me you are a lying, sneaking, controlling bastard who still doesn't trust his wife, no matter what you say to the contrary, apparently I *misinterpreted* the hint. Subtlety isn't my strong point. Sue me."

"Don't you dare twist this and make it about trust," Alec ground out between clenched teeth, taking a step toward her. "You will not risk your safety and well-being. Period. Trust has nothing to do with it."

"Trust has *everything* to do with it." Tessa shouted, throwing her hands in the air. Then she closed her eyes and took a deep breath before continuing. Screeching like a fishwife never solved anything. It simply made it easier to lose the point among the noise. "Look, you just said I will not risk my safety and well-being. What you really mean is *you* won't *allow* me to jeopardize my safety and well-being on what *you* consider a risk. Well, I'm sorry, Alec. I don't need you to think for me."

"Damn it, Tess. I love you. I don't ever want to know how it feels to lose you again. I want you safe. Is that so wrong?" She felt the anger drain out of him as his massive chest expanded and contracted. He raked a hand through his dark curls and began to pace the confines of the small room.

"I know you love me, Alec, but you need to trust me, too." She held up a hand, shaking her head, as he stopped before her and opened his mouth. "Trust is more than believing in my fidelity. Trust means having faith in my ability to think for myself, to know my own strengths and weaknesses, to understand my limitations. Trust is believing in *me*."

"I do believe in you and I'm sorry if I made you feel otherwise. But, you have to understand trust is a two way street. You have to believe in me, too. I've been around longer, have more experience with these bastards, and sometimes I might know what's best even if you disagree. You were damn lucky the only one waiting here when you showed up was a frightened mortal priest. If it had been a *Fallen*...well, I'd rather not think about it."

Tessa's eyes widened as she looked up into the face of this man she loved more than life, realizing he had a point. She stood here demanding he trust her, yet she completely discounted his concerns and his experience. She hadn't trusted him.

"Fair enough. I guess I thought I had something to prove. Clearly, I haven't mastered the suppression of knee jerk reactions quite as well as I gave myself credit for. Of course, you could have taken the time to explain yourself instead of tricking me and disappearing without a word. You acted like a caveman wielding the club of know-it-all machismo." Tessa stepped forward and wrapped her arms around his waist, laying her cheek on the rock hard plane of his chest. "You should work on that."

"I'll try." His warm breath ruffled her hair. "I guess maybe we both have a couple of things to work on, huh? But, it's worth it. *We're* worth it, Tess."

"Yeah, we are," She tipped her head back and smiled up at him. "Besides, constant lack of conflict would get kind of boring after a few decades, don't you think?"

"No doubt," Alec laughed. "Though I don't think there's any danger where we're concerned. Well, Galen and I have determined there was, indeed, something besides Chopin's heart in the urn when the priests here opened it. We also know someone is trying to keep anyone else from finding it. So, as long as you're here *helping*, did you manage to find out anything useful?

"Well, I'm relatively certain the necklace is here somewhere. It's almost like I can feel it. Maybe it's the *Djinni* sensing his own essence is near?" Tessa shook her head and stepped out of Alec's embrace, turning back toward the wall of cabinets. She lifted her arm and extended a finger in the direction of the dim interior of the one she'd been investigating when Alec arrived. "I feel a peculiar pull toward that one. Where's Galen, by the way?"

"He's making sure the priest can't tell anyone we stopped by," Alec replied absently, stepping around Tessa and moving in the direction of the open cabinet. He reached inside, shoved the vestments aside, and began rapping on the wood around the back with his knuckles. Tessa tugged ineffectually on the back of his leather jacket.

"What did you do? He didn't hurt me, you know. He was simply frightened and didn't know what else to do with me. Someone's threatening him."

"And he threatened you," Alec's muffled voice emanated from the depths of the closet. "Which does not sit well with me, even though you had the advantage. And no business being here in the first place." He added as he straightened from the cabinet, and moved to open the open the one next to it, and then the remaining three forming the back wall of the sacristy, tapping around the perimeters as he did with the first one. "He's fine. Galen will find out what he knows and then scrub his memory. He'll wake up in a couple of hours none the worse for wear. I think the back of your cabinet is hollow."

"Meaning?" Tessa reached into the cabinet and laid her hand flat against the back wall, her pulse racing, and waited to see if her gift would provide a hint. Nothing.

"Meaning there should be a solid wall behind it like the others and it seems like there isn't. Could be a niche of some kind covered over during a renovation, the entrance to another room like Michael has at the *Castel*, a hidden passage. Hell, it could be a fluke and mean nothing at all. But, considering your attraction to that particular cabinet, I'm betting we can drop-kick the fluke theory from the mix."

"Seriously, what use is an ability that smacks a girl in the head at the most inopportune moments, and then fails to come through when we need it most?" Tessa withdrew her hand from the cabinet with a frown and brushed her palms down the sides of her jeans. "So, how do we find out what's back there?"

"Well, you *did* point us in the right direction." Alec grasped her shoulders and moved her gently to the side. Then he reached into the cabinet again. "I could power up and blast through it. But, it'd be a shame to destroy all this beautiful old walnut. Or, I could try to fade in and hope there's enough room back there to accommodate me when I reform."

"You're huge, McAllister. I'm smaller, maybe I could..." Tessa began.

"Not a chance," he interrupted. "Of course, there's

one more option. We could do it the easy way." Tessa heard a click, followed by a metallic squeal. Alec stood back from the cabinet and planted his hands on his hips with a wide grin as the back of the cabinet popped open revealing a darkened space beyond. "I could use my superior intelligence and unparalleled powers of deductive reasoning to locate the hidden latch in the carving across the base and simply open the door."

"So, basically, you got lucky?" Tessa smirked.

"I got lucky," he agreed, reaching for her with a chuckle and hauling her against him. Tessa no sooner raised her face to capture his lips when his head snapped up as the unmistakable sensation of shocks racing up and down her spine hit. Galen appeared in the center of the room with a muted pop.

"We've got company," he announced unnecessarily.

"How many?"

"Didn't waste time looking. Set *sigils* around the priest to protect him and headed over here."

Alec's features tightened as he grabbed Tessa's hand, held the vestments aside, and dragged her toward the unknown.

"Wait!" Tessa tugged free and raced to a tall cabinet against the side wall. Yanking open the drawers, she shuffled the contents until she curled her fingers around a couple of long, white taper candles. She shoved some others aside until she located a packet of matches, then she raised her hand triumphantly.

"Good thinking." Galen gently shoved her in Alec's direction, following so closely, he nearly stepped on her heels. Alec grabbed a candle and lit it, then touched it to the wicks of two more and handed one to Tessa and one to Galen, before shoving the matches in his pocket. Then holding his own high in front of him, he reached for Tessa's hand again and pulled her into the passage.

Unnerved by the distorted candlelit shadows dancing along the close confines of the dampened rock walls, Tessa gripped Alec's fingers tightly, and started down the uneven stone stairs. Yes, Alec got lucky finding the passage, but as Galen closed the outer cabinet door, and then pushed the back panel of the cabinet into place with a definitive click, Tessa hoped they weren't on the verge of their luck running out.

Chapter Twenty-One

The further they descended into the earth, the less pronounced the prickling sensation of evil along her spine. Tessa kept her increasing claustrophobia at bay by replaying a Beethoven symphony in her head and concentrating on the solid reality of Alec's fingers wrapped around hers.

"They don't seem to be following us," Galen remarked. "But, I doubt they'll go far. The *sigils* in the rectory will have tipped them off that *Earthbound* are in the neighborhood."

"Probably be waiting when we come up," Alec agreed, stopping to sweep the candle in front of him. Tessa peeked over his shoulder and saw only thick cobwebs dangling from the ceiling and more dusty stairs falling away into the darkness. She swallowed hard and switched to a more uplifting composition by Mozart. "Assuming we go back the way we came. Are you okay?" He brought the candle close and peered into her face.

"Fine," she lied in a breathless voice. "Why?"

"Mozart is your go-to guy when you're nervous." Damn. After ten years of blocking everyone out, she had a tendency to forget she let Alec back in her head.

"It's a little close in here, that's all. It's not as bad as last time, honestly."

Alec brought her hand to his lips and skimmed

them across her knuckles.

"It shouldn't be long now." Giving her fingers a reassuring squeeze, he raised his candle and continued their descent. True to Alec's prediction, within minutes they reached the bottom and found themselves in a small, rough-hewn chamber facing a massive iron door. Alec reached out and rattled the handle, but to no one's surprise, the portal didn't budge.

"Figures," he muttered. "Can nothing be simple?"

"It's not like a locked door can keep us out," Galen chuckled. "We simply fade to the other side. Looks like our only option."

"I know. I'm just not thrilled about going in blind with Tessa along," Alec replied. He sighed and raked his free hand through his hair. "On the other hand, there's no way in heaven or hell I'm leaving her out here alone and unprotected while we check it out."

The giant warrior ran a palm over the tattoos adorning his smooth pate and came away with a handful of shurikens. Then he nodded at Alec. "Okay, McAllister, whip out that new toy you're sporting and let's get on with it."

Tessa regarded Alec in confusion as he released her hand. He handed her his candle and shoved his left sleeve to his elbow, revealing an intricate tattoo on his forearm. After a moment's hesitation, he withdrew a wicked looking dagger from the ink, the blade gleaming with deadly intent in the flickering candlelight.

"Where did you get that?" Tessa gasped.

"Told you we made a pit-stop," Alec shrugged, avoiding her eyes.

"But—" As far as Tessa knew, Michael only bestowed such supernatural weaponry on members of the *Defensori.*

"We'll talk about it later," Alec bit out.

"Don't you think an about-face from scholar to soldier is something worthy of discussion *before* rather than after the fact?" Tessa sniped back.

"Yes, and I said we'll talk about it later." He cupped a hand around her nape and pulled her forward, kissing her hard on the mouth. "Nothing's been decided. Now, be a good girl and hold onto the candles so Galen and I can keep our hands free."

Tessa clutched her sputtering taper, as well as Alec's, as Galen blew his out and tossed it to the floor. He transferred half of the steel throwing stars to his other hand, and stepped around her to Alec's side.

"Tess, you stay behind Alec and me until we see what we're dealing with," Galen directed. "We fade on three. One, two, three…"

Tessa materialized on the other side of the door and found herself alone in a sealed room surrounded by deathly quiet.

"Alec?"

She reached out to him first on their private wavelength, and then on the open channel all *Earthbound* used, but neither he nor Galen replied. Where could they be? Alec would never leave her alone down here deliberately. Did the *Djinni* sense the proximity of the piece of himself she carried, and allow entry to her alone? Did the creature actually wield that kind of power even though trapped? Not a comforting thought. Her chest tightened and her lungs struggled to draw in the thick, age-stale air. Heart racing, she held the candles aloft and examined the small room more closely. It looked as though it hadn't been disturbed in years. The smart move would be to return to the other side and locate Alec and Galen. But, a force stronger than her common sense drew her like iron filings to a magnet toward the heavy wooden table against the opposite wall. The black metal box sitting in the middle of its dust covered top pulsed with a life of its own in the dancing shadows cast by the flickering candlelight.

Tipping the tapers, she dripped the melted wax onto the tabletop, then stuck the bases in the cooling puddle, creating a makeshift candle stand. Sucking in a shaky breath, she caught her lower lip between her teeth, and held her hands over the box. She should leave this place and find Alec. He must be frantic. But, they came for the necklace, right? Shouldn't she at least see if they were right, or if this entire expedition was a waste of time? *Open it, open it.* The thought welled up, unbidden, from the deepest recesses of her mind, a thought not her own. Alec, she must find Alec. But, the trapped *Djinni*, was here. She knew it as well as she knew her own name. And she could free him. It would only take a minute.

Tessa flipped open the lid and snatched the necklace from its resting place. A tortured scream fractured the silence the moment she curled her fingers around the filigree cage and came in contact with the smooth, cold stone. Memories crashed over her with the force of a monsoon. Rage, desperation, betrayal, and torment drowned her in suffocating darkness. Held captive by the *Djinni's* memories, her senses screamed as she struggled to rise to the surface and free herself. The pressure threatened to split her head in two as the *Djinni* tore free of her consciousness to reunite the pieces of his own. The searing pain vanquished the visions, and left her panting on the floor, gasping for breath, her fingers still locked around the pendant. She pressed her other hand to her forehead and struggled to her feet, wondering if the dull pounding she heard came from within her head. She gripped the edge of the table, thankful for the support. It was the only thing preventing her from face-planting when the *Djinni* stepped from the shadows and smiled.

"Well, little angel, I believe I owe you both my thanks and my apologies."

****

Alec hit the stone floor with the force of a cannon blast.

He shook his head to clear it, slapped his dagger against his forearm, and climbed to his feet in the darkness. He heard a scuffling to his right, and then the space lit with an eerie blue glow emanating from Galen's palms. Alec glanced around wildly, his heart climbing into his throat. "Tess? Where's Tessa?"

"Hell-forged steel. The door and walls must be laced with it. Guess we probably should have checked first." Galen scooped his abandoned candle from the floor. "Lot less painful that way. Got a match?"

Alec dug them out of his pocket and tossed them to Galen. "Okay, hell-forged steel. We can't fade through it, so where the hell is my wife?"

"Your wife isn't *Earthbound*. My guess is, she's on the other side of the door." Galen struck a match and the candle flared to life as the glow from his palms faded. He brushed the dust from his jeans, then bent to scoop his throwing stars from the floor where they'd scattered when he landed. He returned all except one into the ink on his scalp, then scraped the edge of the remaining one along the surface of the door. He arched a brow at Alec when the friction produced sparks of both red and blue. "Not only hell-forged, but heaven-forged, too. Smelted in iron. Whoever constructed this wanted to make damn sure no one—*Earthbound, Fallen,* or *Djinn*—got in. Or out. Telepathy won't penetrate it, either. Don't get your shorts in a knot. Tessa is an intelligent woman. As soon as she realizes we didn't get through, she'll be back."

"She's had plenty of time to realize it," Alec croaked, advancing to run his hands over the door. Anything—or anyone—could be on the other side. He couldn't feel Tessa, couldn't sense her. He should have demanded she return to his mother's. Angry and hurt he could fix. Dead might be a bit trickier. "We aren't standing here with our thumbs up our asses waiting for her to reappear. There has to be a way to breach this."

"I don't think so," Galen grunted, holding the candle close to examine the perimeter of the portal. "Whoever put this together did a pretty thorough job. I didn't go straight through the door. The walls are laced with the stuff, too."

"Well, I didn't get her back to lose her again," Alec shot back, slamming his fist impotently against the barrier. He mopped at his sweaty forehead with his sleeve and planted his hands on his hips, the better to conceal their trembling. He couldn't help Tessa if he let the fear control him. *Think, McAllister.* With his head cocked to the side, Alec watched Galen continue to run his palms around the doorframe, searching for any weakness. Something about the scene struck a familiar chord. The answer came courtesy of a flashback to his sister-in-law Katrina's basement and a time when

Jacques Rapier held Kassian's wife hostage in a series of tunnels beneath the mountains. Kat's cousin, a powerful witch, cast a spell on the entrances, forcing Alec, his brother, and Luca to stand helpless, unable to breach the magic. When they couldn't find a way through it, they went around it.

"You said the walls are laced with hell-forged, so it's mixed with stone?" Alec clapped a hand on Galen's shoulder and pulled him away from the door. He rubbed his palms together until they glowed, then directed a blast of blue white energy at the wall beside the doorway, giving a satisfied grunt as it cracked and rumbled. "What if we can weaken the walls around the door enough to blow it out?"

"Not a horrible idea. In fact, it could work." Galen rubbed a hand over the back of his neck as Alec directed another blast at the same area as the first. Dirt and tiny fragments of stone trickled from the spot, and the ceiling creaked overhead. "Then again, it could bring the whole place down on top of us...and Tessa."

"You have a better idea?" Alec hesitated, his gut tensing. He had no concern for his own well-being, but until he clapped eyes on her, he had no way of knowing Tessa's current situation. If the tunnel collapsed and anything impeded her ability to fade, his plan could easily bury her alive.

"Well, not yet, but—" Both men froze. Galen's head swiveled and locked on Alec, whose muscles bunched into apprehensive knots as a muffled scream from beyond the door pierced the silence. Tessa's scream. Galen tossed the candle to the floor, where it sputtered and died. Then he quickly buffed his palms and directed his energy at the wall. "Hey, what the hell.

A bad plan beats no plan, yeah? You stay left, I'll blast right."

Alec knuckled his burning eyes, and squinted through the murky light. He mentally reached out to Tessa over and over as he and Galen worked, every sense straining to discern the slightest whisper of response. Nothing. His throat ached and his eyes watered, temporarily clearing the grit from his vision. The door stood as solid as the Rock of Gibraltar, and only the superficial facing of the wall crumbled. Mouth dry, chest tight, he kicked at the pile of pulverized stone littering the floor, and swore loudly. They weren't getting anywhere.

"Maybe it's time to consider going to plan B," Galen croaked, bending to hug his knees as a fit of coughing seized him.

"You got a plan B?" Alec asked.

"Not yet, but I'm working on it," he rasped.

"Then we keep going." Alec directed another blast of energy at the stubborn rock. Dirt rained down from the groaning ceiling like confetti.

Galen's brow pleated as he glanced up. "Not sure that's the best option."

Alec followed the other man's gaze. An irregular crack split the rock ceiling, spanning half the distance from the doorway to the bottom of the stairs. He swallowed hard and rolled his stiffened shoulders. "It's the only option."

"Alec—"

"I know. But, I'm not leaving without Tessa, no matter what happens. This isn't your problem, Galen. Get yourself out before I bring the whole damn thing down on our heads." Alec rubbed his palms together and aimed them at the wall beside the door. "Seriously, no hard feelings."

"Told you before, no one goes in alone. And no one gets left behind. Not even stubborn assholes."

"Yet you'd leave Tessa behind?" Alec clenched his jaw until his teeth ached, fixing a glare on the bald warrior.

"Absolutely not. Just need to figure out an alternate plan. But, since you're hell-bent on this one..." Galen scraped his hands together and focused them on the same area Alec targeted. "Let's concentrate both our energies on one spot and see if we can make a dent. And for the record, you're going to owe me big time for the massive headache and assorted broken bones I foresee in my immediate future."

The force of the combined blast sent large chunks of stone spewing from the wall, and revealed the tight cross-hatch of metal strips woven in concrete beneath. Alec took his first full breath since Tessa disappeared. One tiny chink, one pinhole of penetration was all he needed to touch her mind and make sure she was safe. "Again."

The second dual blast enlarged the hole. It also widened the fissure above them, raining buckets of dirt and rubble on their heads. An ominous rumble sounded deep within the rock, and the room shook as the crack widened and deepened. His eyes locked on Galen's and he knew the warrior's alarmed expression matched the one he must be wearing.

"Alec?" Alec spun in disbelief. There stood Tessa, an amber stone caged in metal dangling from the heavy chain around her slender neck, her brow pleated in a perplexed expression. As his heart kicked him in the ribs, her wide, blue eyes shot toward the ceiling when the earth groaned. The crack expanded, and a fine layer of dust filtered down to powder her bright curls. "Well, that can't be good."

"Out!" Galen roared, diving to grab Tessa with one hand and snagging a handful of Alec's shirt with the other. They dematerialized as the ceiling shuddered and thundered down on top of them, reappearing a heartbeat later in a dusty heap on the floor of the sacristy.

Chapter Twenty-Two

Conscious of the pin-prick shocks racing along his spine confirming their company remained, Alec extricated himself from the tangle of limbs and climbed to his feet. He reached down and grasped Tessa's outstretched hand, and pulled her up against him. Now, with her safely in his arms, he couldn't decide whether to kiss her senseless, or kick her sweetly rounded ass.

"Contessa McAllister, if you ever scare me like that again—"

"For the love of...Alec, don't you think you're overreacting? It was only a few minutes—"

"More than a few," he ground out. It felt like hours.

"Seriously? I didn't realize. I'm sorry, Alec." Tessa brushed the hair from his forehead, then cupped his cheek. "Truly."

He gazed into her bright blue eyes and realized he could think of far better things to do with her magnificent ass than kick it. Kiss her senseless, he decided. As soon as they wrapped up this mess and he got her alone. Of course, at the first opportunity he still planned a stern lecture on consideration, common sense, and never again taking three centuries off her husband's life.

"And look," she smiled brightly, holding up the pendant and ignoring his surly attitude. "We did it!"

"Be careful with than damn thing." Alec snatched

it from her fingers. The stone pulsed with a life and light of its own. "Look what happened last time you touched it."

"No, it's all right. I admit, Mekonnen's exit from my psyche turned out to be a bit more uncomfortable than I anticipated, but now he's reunited the pieces of himself and is whole again. He promised it wouldn't hurt this time."

"Mekonnen?" Alec asked, shifting his attention to Galen.

The hulking *Defensori* rose to his feet in one fluid motion, nodded, then stepped to the doorway leading out to the church. He palmed a shuriken from his scalp and twitched back the heavy velvet curtain.

Alec's *Earthbound* senses continued to warn him evil lurked nearby, but whoever waited hadn't yet entered the church. He returned his attention to his wife. "So, where is he?"

"In here." She filched the caged stone from Alec's unresisting fingers. "Wearing him was the only way to bring him out with me." She wedged a finger between the bars of intricately twisted metal to touch the amber jewel before Alec could stop her. He watched in amazement as a thick, green haze streamed from the gem, coalescing into a slim, well-dressed mocha-skinned man. Dark eyes twinkling, he pressed his palms together under the neatly trimmed salt-and-pepper beard tracing his jawline, and bowed his head to Tessa.

"My thanks once again, little angel."

"My pleasure, Mekonnen. This is my husband, Alec."

"Ah, yes. I recognize you," the *Djinni* nodded. "I'm still assimilating the rogue piece of my essence, but you were such a presence in Tessa's mind these many years, I feel I know you."

"I see," Alec replied uncomfortably, not seeing at all. Had the *Djinni* been privy to all of Tessa's thoughts? He didn't much care for that idea. On the other hand, she must have thought about him quite a bit over the years. That idea suited him fine.

"And this is our friend…" Tessa waved the arm not clutching Alec's waist toward the silent warrior keeping watch.

"Galen," the *Djinni* finished for her. The muscles in Galen's shoulders bunched visibly.

"Exactly. He's the one who discovered you in my mind and helped us find you," Tessa smiled.

"Of course he did," Mekonnen observed dryly. "You're looking well, nephew."

"Wait, what? *Nephew?*" Alec stared.

Galen released the curtain, then turned slowly, crossing his arms over his massive chest. "It's been a long time, uncle."

"Indeed it has. Still determinedly clinging to your father's world, I see."

"We've traveled this road many times, and we'll always end up at the same destination. Give it a rest."

"Your mother misses you," the older man cajoled.

"You've been away a long time, Mekonnen. Your kingdom is changed." Galen's green eyes flashed and his lips thinned. "My mother is dead."

Mekonnen paled and his fingers curled into fists at his sides. "Who?"

"I think we both know the answer."

"You have proof?"

"I don't need proof, just an opportunity."

"Well, perhaps that can be arranged." The old *Djinni* closed his eyes and sucked in a deep breath through his nose. His eyes snapped open and fixed on the door. "Sooner rather than later. We're about to have company. Angel, put the necklace on, please."

Who did this guy think he was, anyway? Alec opened his mouth to protest, but Tessa dutifully released Alec and dropped the chain over her head. Mekonnen waved a hand over the stone and it pulsed with light exactly as it did while he resided inside. The *Djinni* gazed into Tessa's eyes for several seconds until she nodded shortly.

"Get out of my wife's head, old man," Alec growled.

"Galen," the elder turned his attention to his kinsman. Galen strode across the room and took up a position next to Alec, and behind Tessa. "You know what to do, nephew?" Galen nodded, his jaw tight.

"Would someone like to tell me what the hell is going on?" Alec growled.

"In a nutshell? I'll take out the *animorti* who will almost certainly come in first. Tessa and the necklace will then serve as a diversion. While the bastard is occupied, Mekonnen will attempt to take the sonofabitch down. *Djinn* are nearly impossible to kill, unless they take human form," Galen said through stiff lips. "Even then, there's a chance they'll escape the mortal vessel prior to its death. Keep your dagger handy. If Mekonnen fails, we'll have to take the bastard out before he exits the host body."

"And if we don't?"

Galen's head swiveled and his eyes narrowed on Alec. "It's best if we do."

"Okay, I've heard enough. Tessa is leaving. Now." Alec announced, holding out his hand. "Give me the necklace. I'll be the diversion."

Tessa laid a hand on his chest and turned the full force of her magnificent blue eyes on him.

"Alec, I can do this. Mekonnen won't let him hurt me. Galen won't let him hurt me. And you most certainly won't let him hurt me. I love you, and I trust you to keep me safe. The question is, can you trust me?"

"Trust has nothing to do with it," he snapped. Tessa quirked a brow and the corners of her lips lifted. Didn't they have this conversation before? What had she said? Trust meant having faith in her ability to think for herself, to know her own strengths and weaknesses, to understand her limitations. Trust meant believing in her. Alec huffed out a breath and pulled her into his arms, pressing his lips to her bright curls. "I do trust you, Tess. It's the rest of the world I have a problem with." He glared at the *Djinni* and drew his dagger from the ink on his arm. "Just so we're clear. She is the most important thing in this room. If this plan goes south, get her out of here no matter what."

"I owe her my life, and I will sacrifice it to keep her safe. You have my word." Mekonnen bowed his head. Then he cocked it to the side at the sound of footsteps echoing on the marble floor of the church. "And so it begins. Stand where he can see the necklace immediately, little angel. Places, everyone."

The *Djinni* dissolved into a wisp of faint gray smoke, invisible for all intents and purposes, and rose to hover over the doorway. Galen stood beside Alec, absently spinning a shuriken between the fingers of each hand. Tessa positioned herself in front of them, clenching and unclenching her hands at her sides, careful to give Galen enough space to launch his weapons. Alec tightened his grip on his dagger. Allowing Tessa to stand front and center flew in the face of every protective instinct he possessed, and his gut clenched as he resisted the urge to shove her behind him. He hoped Mekonnen would remain true to his word if all hell broke loose. Luca believed even presumably good *Djinn* were suspect. Still, Galen apparently claimed more *Djinn* ancestry than anyone guessed, and Alec never knew him to be anything less than honorable. There were clearly exceptions to every rule.

"Any idea who we're planning to kill?" Alec sent the question to Tessa's mind, while Galen's attention remained riveted on the door.

"Mekonnen's brother, Ejigu. Taking advantage of the Nazis' fascination with the occult, he saw a golden opportunity to remove his brother from his throne in the realm of the Djinn and trap him on this plane. In exchange for his promise to finish the tunnels, the Nazis helped him conjure and capture Mekonnen. But, after the necklace was stolen, he realized trapping his brother and entrusting the trap to humans wouldn't do. He needed to ensure Mekonnen could never be released from his prison and reclaim his position, so he concocted a plan to ensure his brother's eternal captivity. Posing as an expert in demonology, he persuaded the priests here to seal the necklace in an impenetrable chamber no one could breach by convincing them the stone contained a powerful and malevolent fiend intent on helping the Nazis achieve

world domination. We got the location right, but the motivation all wrong."

"Trapping the Djinni was never about saving the Reich, it was a political coup to topple a Djinn king." Alec shook his head. *"I guess that explains the room's design to keep out Fallen, Earthbound, and Djinn alike. Of course, Ejigu didn't count on a beautiful Principalitie. If he's a Djinni and not a Fallen, where do the animorti come in?"*

"He's got friends in low places."

"Figures. So, you freed a Djinni, had his essence ripped from your brain, got this whole story, and honestly believed you were only gone a couple of minutes?"

"Hey, I said I was sor—" Tessa halted in mid-thought as the curtain twitched and two *animorti* slipped inside the sacristy.

Before the heavy fabric settled into place, with preternatural speed, Galen whipped two deadly shurikens across the room. The *Fallen* servants' mouths dropped open right before they exploded like balloons filled with motor oil, spraying foul black goop everywhere.

"That's revolting." Tessa shuddered. Alec couldn't disagree, but he saw it often enough to be immune. He slipped his free hand beneath Tessa's heavy mane and cupped the back of her neck, his fingertips soothing the tense knots.

"Their reward for allowing greed to trump common sense. Poor bastards think aligning themselves with the Fallen makes them special. All it makes them is cannon fodder."

Alec froze as footsteps shuffled to a halt beyond

the drape. Showtime. He gave Tessa's neck a gentle squeeze, and dropped his hand back to his side, curling it into a fist.

"If something goes wrong, get yourself out of here, no matter what. I need you to promise me you'll worry about yourself, so I don't have to."

Tessa nodded. *"I promise. I love you, Alec."*

"I love you more. Be ready for anything."

Tessa nodded again, mentally preparing herself. But, nothing could have prepared her for the man who swept aside the dusty velvet and stepped into the room. Tears sprang to her eyes, and her heart leapt into her throat, as she locked her knees to avoid collapsing to the floor.

"Steady, Tess," Galen urged mentally. *"You know that's not your father. The bastard's trying to keep us off balance."*

Incapable of an immediate response, Tessa blinked rapidly and nodded. Of course she knew, but for one heart-stopping moment she'd believed. A low growl emanated from her husband as Alec's hand touched the small of her back. She felt the rage percolating in his gut, his overwhelming need to protect her from this grief.

"It's okay," she reassured Alec and Galen. She squared her shoulders and sucked in a fortifying breath. She needed to pull herself together before the man she loved did something tragically stupid on her behalf. *"I'm okay."*

"Contessa, my precious one," the imposter crooned, opening his arms.

"Is impersonating a dead man for shock value the best trick you've got, Ejigu?" Tessa spat with more courage than she felt. Frankly, given the tightness in her throat, it surprised her she could speak at all. "I'm afraid you'll have to do better than that. You're pathetic."

"He always did have more bravado than brains," Galen snickered, advancing to draw level on Tessa's right as Alec moved forward on the left. "Isn't that right, *uncle*?"

"Knowing Bartolucci's daughter married an *Earthbound*, I guess I should have expected a *Defensori*, namely *you*, might be tagging along. Tell me, *nephew*, have there been any leads on your dear mother's whereabouts?" The hateful sneer that contorted the doppelganger's features broke the spell. Tessa no longer saw any resemblance to her beloved father. Galen stiffened beside her.

"Steady, Galen. The bastard's trying to keep us off balance." Tessa nudged the tense *Defensori* with her elbow, and threw his advice back at him.

"Leave my mother out of this. We all know she's not the reason you're here," Galen snarled.

"No, but since there are two of you and one of me, I find myself at an unexpected disadvantage." His gaze fixed on the pendant pulsing between Tessa's breasts. "Perhaps we can work a deal? The necklace in exchange for information about your mother."

"You were right about his lack of brains, Galen. Apparently your uncle can't count. It's three against one by my estimation," Tessa forced her stiff lips into an amused grin. Then she forked two fingers at her eyes. "And I'm up here, Ejigu."

"Why must you poke the bear, Tess?" Alec sighed in her head.

"Because he doesn't consider me a threat. He has no idea I'm the fourth in this little welcoming quartet. It's to our advantage to keep it that way. Besides, he's cruel and I don't like him." Tessa swore she heard Alec's eyes roll.

"How charming. The little rose has thorns. Sorry to disillusion you, sweetheart, but my interest is solely in your choice of accessories."

"This old thing?" Tessa wrapped her fingers around the pendant and lifted it away from her chest and toward the *Djinni*, batting her eyes for effect. She let the pendant drop against her body and steeled her voice. "You want it, Ejigu? Come and get it."

"Poke, poke, poke," Alec grumbled.

Ejigu's eyes narrowed and he licked his lips in anticipation. His gaze darted between Galen and Alec, who remained perfectly still as he cautiously took one step, and then another. *Come on, come on,* Tessa coaxed silently. One more step gave Mekonnen enough room to materialize behind his brother, a wicked looking scimitar raised high over his head. He drove the curved blade into Ejigu's back before the evil *Djinni* knew what hit him, powering steel through flesh until the point projected from the chest. Ejigu reached toward Tessa, as the light left the eyes, and the body crumpled to the floor.

Sheer determination kept her standing as pain threatened to rip her in two. Her head knew it wasn't her father, but the uncanny likeness persuaded her heart she was losing him all over again. Tessa squeezed her eyes shut and turned her face away, unable to witness his death a second time. Galen dropped a comforting had on her shoulder, and Alec hauled her against his side as helpless sobs wracked her.

"It's okay, baby. It's over," Alec whispered into her hair.

She cracked open her eyes and stared at the now prone and lifeless body, puzzled by the wisps of thick, black vapor rising from the wound near the hilt of the sword. Mekonnen's alarmed shout penetrated her cloud of grief. The *Djinni* was escaping, and she knew what she needed to do.

As the mist thickened, Tessa wrenched free of both men, and yanked the heavy chain over her head. Curling her fingers around the cage, she jammed them between the iron bars, touching as much of the stone as she possibly could. Then she stepped forward and plunged her hand into the heart of the mist.

The agony was instantaneous. Mekonnen entered the trap willingly, knowing she intended to free him. He produced barely a frisson of awareness on the edge of Tessa's consciousness as he passed through her gifted fingers and into the stone. Ejigu on the other hand, facing certain annihilation, battled captivity with all the weapons he could muster. Invading every part of her consciousness, he dragged her into a soul-sucking darkness worse than any nightmare she ever experienced. Unspeakable horrors reflected like sharp shattered glass in the vast nothingness of the endless obscurity she fought to resist. Reality became darkness, and darkness became reality. Ejigu's strength exceeded hers. She would lose this fight. Lose herself. Lose everything. *Alec.* Cold assaulted her. She floated in inky blackness on an endless sea.

Hopeless.

Alone.

Drowning.

"I love you, Alec." A frantic plea. A final farewell.

A pinhole of light, tiny and dim, flickered in the emptiness.

"Tessa! Fight!"

The raw anguish in Alec's voice pulled her head above the water.

"Here, I'm here." Her weakened mind offered a desperate response so faint and indistinct, Tessa barely heard it herself. But, Alec heard. His love invaded her mind, wrapped around her like a warm blanket, and hauled her from the deep well of endless nothingness. She sighed in relief.

"Galen!" Alec called.

Immediately, the pinhole expanded, cracks radiated from the margins, and bursts of light pierced the darkness. Galen's consciousness arrived, closely followed by Mekonnen. The gloom receded. For the first time since plunging her hand into the mist, Tessa felt the welcome pressure of Alec's arms around her.

"It's getting crowded in here," she whispered.

"The more the merrier," Galen cracked.

"Rest, little angel," Mekonnen said. Cool fingers stroked her brow. *"You fought valiantly. Now it's our turn. Alec, on my signal, tear that damn thing from her hand. Let's end this."*

Ejigu's desperate howls and shrieks of denial sent jolts of pain ricocheting inside Tessa's skull as Galen and his uncle used their combined magic to force the evil *Djinni* out of her mind and into the trap.

"Now!"

Just when Tessa feared her head might explode, metal scraped her fingers, stinging and abrading skin, as

Alec tore the pendant from her grasp. The wailing ceased, and blessed silence descended.

****

"Tess, c'mon, honey, wake up." Alec's voice sounded faint and far away, and more than a little strained. Tessa struggled through the cottony layers of exhaustion to find his pale, worried face hovering above her. Galen, over Alec's left shoulder, and Mekonnen, over his right, looked no less concerned.

"You found me," Tessa whispered with a smile. The tense lines in his face eased.

"I will always find you," Alec promised, pressing his lips to hers. "And after I kiss you senseless, I will kick your lovely ass."

Chapter Twenty-Three

"You are a shameless monopolizer of babies," Callista pouted, reaching for her daughter in vain. Alec tucked the pink bundle more securely in the crook of his arm, refusing to surrender the baby to her mother. Foiled, Calli turned her attention to Tessa. "I still say if you free a *Djinni*, he owes you a wish. I saw this old show once—."

"You watch entirely too much television," Alec interrupted his sister with a grin. "And we're leaving soon, so back off and let me enjoy my niece. It might be a while before I see her again."

"Seriously, Alec, Kentucky?" Luca arched a brow. "All rolling green hills and bucolic serenity. You'll be stir crazy in no time. I give you a month, tops."

"Tessa loves teaching there," Alec replied with a shrug. "And since I'll still be working for Michael, as well as filling in *per diem* as a *Defensori*—because some people, you know, demand paternity leave—we'll travel often enough. But, we'll also have an actual home base to come back to. I think it's about time, don't you?" He winked at Tessa.

"Past time, I'd say," Tessa concurred, crossing the room to slip her arm through Alec's and gaze at the wondrous and perfect miniature person held so tenderly in his arms. "But, as I've told you more than once, my home is wherever you are. You need to come for a visit,

Luca. You might discover you actually enjoy those rolling green hills and a little bucolic serenity."

Baby Lilliana stared back at Tessa from enormous eyes the same brilliant blue as her mother's, set in identical delicate features. From Luca, the tiny girl inherited the faint cleft in her chin, and her silky fair hair. But, then she smiled, and her deep dimples were pure Alec. Tessa's breath caught in her throat imagining Alec cradling a child of his own.

"I think I want ten," Alec laughed, reading her mind.

Heaven knows, they had enough room for ten children in the enormous white clapboard farmhouse Alec bought and renovated. Close to the conservatory, with an enormous wrap around porch, and oozing with character and charm, Tessa fell in love with the place on sight. After she added the pieces of her father's she decided to keep, it truly was everything she'd ever dreamed of. Alec promised her a home, and he delivered.

"Let's start with one and see how it goes." Tessa laughed at Alec and cocked her head at her brother-in-law. "Really, you all should come. We've plenty of space, and when Lilliana gets a bit older, there's even room for a pony."

"Perhaps a little tranquility *would* be pleasant. Of course, I'd miss my wife. She and tranquility have never met." Callista tugged a pillow from behind her back and whipped it at her husband's head.

Luca caught it without even glancing in her direction. Then he crossed to the sofa, shoved the pillow behind her neck, and dropped down next to her. He reached for Callista's hand, brushed his lips across her knuckles, and then rested their entwined fingers on his thigh.

Tessa shook her head. She still had trouble reconciling this domestic side of the Ice Warrior with the Luca she knew, but decided she liked it.

"So, a call-in *Defensori?* That's a first," Luca remarked. "You fight as well as anyone, Alec. Why limit yourself? A man with your strength and skill is valuable."

"Funny, it's what I always thought I wanted. It felt like *not* enlisting made me…less." Alec mused. Then his face split in a wide grin. "Sure, I can fight as well as any of you, and I'm more than willing to step in when needed. But, the fact is, I can research rings around all of you and my research has pulled your ass out of more than one sticky situation."

"And that's a skill no less valuable. I'm happy you finally figured out what the rest of us have always known." Luca grinned. "We don't call you the Riddle King for nothing."

"Someone has to do the thinking," a deep voice interjected from the doorway.

"Michael." Tessa smiled, slipping her arm from Alec's, and stepped into the Archangel's embrace. "I hoped we'd see you before we left. I know you rarely leave Rome, and I'm not sure how long it will be before we come back."

"Kentucky." Michael's lips thinned and twisted. "I heard."

"What on earth do you all have against Kentucky?" Tessa threw her hands in the air. "It's beautiful there!"

"It's so…tranquil," Michael muttered.

"All the more reason for you to visit," Tessa

teased. "All war and no play make Michael a cranky archangel."

"I didn't start the battle, Contessa. But, make no mistake. I *will* finish it. It's taken centuries, and it may take centuries more, but evil will not prevail. And I'm not cranky."

Tessa shook her head as Michael strode across the room to peer at Lilliana. "She's absolutely lovely Callista, in spite of her paternity," he said. "Ah, well, one can't pick one's relatives."

"Speaking of relatives, I assume you knew Galen isn't simply descended from a *Djinni,* but is half *Djinn* himself?" Alec asked.

"Of course, I knew. It's my business to know. He's also half *Earthbound,* and that's the side he chose to embrace." Michael waggled a finger near the baby's nose, his face lighting with a megawatt smile when she curled her tiny fingers around it and held fast. "He's planning to spend some time with Mekonnen and his family in the *Djinn* realm, and then he'll be back to work."

"Would you like to hold her?" Callista asked softly.

Michael straightened, his eyes widening. Then the corners of his lips lifted. "Why, yes. I would."

"I don't think—" Luca half rose from the sofa, alarm flitting across his features.

"Sit down, Fiorelli," Michael snapped. "I am a military commander, have directed the fight against evil on earth for millennia, signaled the end of plagues, and helped cast Lucifer from the heavens. I think I can handle a six pound baby." Alec glanced at his sister, who bit back a smile, then nodded serenely. Supporting

Lilliana's downy head, he carefully transferred the pink-swathed little body into the thick arms of the Archangel.

"And don't forget modest, Your Grace," Luca groused, settling back near his wife. "You're incredibly modest."

"Facts are facts." Michael shrugged. He lowered his face to the baby's, smiling delightedly when she grabbed a handful of his golden curls.

"Is he *cooing*?" Alec stage whispered, his mouth dropping open.

"No," Tessa smiled. "He's communicating with her. It's an Archangel thing. I can't speak the language, but thanks to my *Principalitie* heritage, I can understand it."

Michael glanced up with a frown. "Lilliana and I are having a private conversation, Contessa. Don't feel compelled to translate, if you get my drift."

"He warned her to never break her father's heart," Tessa continued in a choked voice, as though he hadn't spoken. Hot tears pricked the backs of her lids. She blinked them away and turned toward the others. Michael might be a prince of the heavens and rule his army with an iron fist, but he'd always treated her like a beloved niece. Everyone, even Archangels, made poor decisions and did stupid things in the name of love. Tessa could certainly attest to that fact. They shouldn't be judged for them forever. Michael would never explain himself to his men, or ask them to cut him some slack concerning his folly. But, Tessa could. "A father will do anything for love of a daughter, even foolish, forbidden things that bite him in the ass for centuries. He told me the same thing once upon a time. I didn't understand it then."

"As I recall, I also admonished you on more than one occasion to respect your elders. Apparently, *that* caveat continues to fall on deaf ears," Michael muttered in a gruff tone. He cleared his throat, straightened, and handed Lilliana to her mother. "Furthermore, I told her she's beautiful, and special, and will someday accomplish great things."

"That should be obvious to everyone." Madge stepped from the bottom of the stairs and breezed into the parlor in a cloud of designer fragrance. "She *is* my grand-daughter, after all."

"You look lovely, Mother." Callista smiled.

"What's the occasion?" Alec asked.

"I'm going out for an early dinner," Madge replied airily, slipping her hand into the crook of Michael's arm. "I finally persuaded Michael to crawl out of that cold pile of stone he holes up in."

"You're going to dinner with *him*?" Alec gasped, his jaw hitting the floor. Luca wore a similar expression. Tessa swallowed a giggle when color stained Michael's high cheekbones. Flustered was a completely new look for him.

"Magdalena needs to eat. I need to eat. Why shouldn't we eat together?" Michael said. "You and Contessa are leaving presently. In fact," He ducked his head to glance through the front window. "Your car just pulled up out front. And I'm sure Luca and Callista would appreciate some alone time with Lilliana."

"But—"

"Off you go, dears." Madge released the Archangel, and embraced Tessa. Then she turned and wrapped her arms around Alec, before pushing them both gently in the direction of the front door. "I love you. Have a safe flight, and text me when you land."

"Here's your hat, what's your hurry," Alec muttered, scooping his duffle bag from the floor of the foyer and slinging Tessa's backpack over his arm.

"Come see us soon," Tessa called as Alec pulled the door closed.

****

"What were you thinking?" Tessa yawned, slipping her backpack from her shoulders inside the front door and flicking on the lights. "Two layovers before we even left Europe. Why didn't you book a non-stop flight?"

"None available." Alec shrugged, dropping the rest of their bags next to hers. He stretched his arms over his head until his back gave a satisfactory crack, then gathered Tessa in his arms and rested his chin on top of her head. "And we're home now, right?"

"Yes, we are." Tessa yawned again. "Home. It has a nice ring, doesn't it? Are you sure about this? I mean, *I* love it, but I know you prefer the city."

"I prefer wherever you are, Tess. Besides, I still have the apartments in New York and Paris, and we'll visit my mother in Rome. We aren't exactly stranded in the middle of nowhere," Alec chuckled.

"True. And Kassian and his wife will be here for a visit next week. I can't wait to see him and meet Katrina. Any woman who can keep your brother in line must be pretty special," Tessa laughed.

"Or half crazy. But, yeah, you'll love her." Alec squinted down the darkened hallway leading to the kitchen, trying to discern any hint of movement through the new French doors leading out to the patio.

"*Everything ready?*" He sent the message on the wavelength used exclusively by *Defensori*.

"*Been ready for two hours. Just waiting on you, brother. Don't think that second layover was strictly necessary,*" Kassian responded dryly. Alec suppressed the urge to whoop. He pressed his lips to Tessa's forehead instead. *Damn, he actually pulled it off.*

"I can't wait to hop in the shower and become close personal friends with our new mattress." Tessa propped her chin on his chest and gazed up at him. Her lids drooped with fatigue, and he suffered a momentary pang of guilt. Maybe planning this after sixteen hours of traveling hadn't been the best idea. Nothing could erase the pain he caused her all those years ago, but now that they'd been gifted with a second chance, he never intended to let a day go by taking her love for granted again.

"Let's check out the back deck before we go up. I want to make sure the contractor finished everything," Alec suggested, releasing her from his arms. He grabbed her hand and tugged her down the hall in the direction of the darkened kitchen.

"Alec, it's pitch black outside," Tessa moaned, dragging her feet. "Can't it wait until tomorrow? Preferably sometime after noon, since I have no intention of crawling out of bed until at least lunchtime."

"Humor me." Alec pulled her along behind him, then unlatched and slid open the door.

"*Now.*"

He stepped aside, allowing Tessa to precede him. His heart felt full enough to burst as she turned to him, her eyes widened and lips parted in surprise. Opposite the deck, a full orchestra with Tessa's excited students scattered among them, sat in a semicircle with instruments poised. Galen and Mekonnen stepped from the darkness, revealing the source of the magic illuminating the trees with twinkling fairy lights. His mother and Michael, Kassian and Kat, Luca and Callista all sat on the far side of the deck, observing her reaction with wide grins. Baby Lilliana squirmed and squawked in her father's arms.

"As I remember, your symphony is lovely enough to soothe a wild beast," Luca observed laconically. "Fortunate, as it seems a certain member of your audience is getting restless,"

"My symphony?" Tessa whispered in a husky voice, turning to Alec with tear bright eyes. "You did all this? How?"

"I know it's not the Royal Festival Hall, and it's ten years overdue—" Alec began. She pressed her fingers to his lips, halting his words.

"It's perfect." Tessa croaked in a husky voice. She stepped into his arms and buried her face in his chest. Alec wrapped his arms around his wife, drawing her shuddering frame against him, struggling to find the words. He blinked away moisture and his throat tightened.

"If people learn from their mistakes, I should be a freaking genius by now," he whispered into her hair. "Not everyone gets a second chance. And while it's infinitely better to get it right the first time, I've learned my lesson. I won't squander it. I promise. I love you, Tessa."

"I love you, too," Tessa sniffed, stretching up on her toes to press her lips to his. "Calli was right, you know. Mekonnen did offer me a wish to repay me for his freedom. I turned him down."

"Why?"

"You gave me your heart, you gave me a home." Tessa looked beyond him at their audience, and the tears coursed freely down her cheeks as she returned her gaze to his. "You gave me a family. And now this…" The musicians took up their instruments and the opening strains of the overture—the melody she told Alec she heard in her mind the very first time she saw him—filled the night air. Tessa shook her head, reaching up to cup his cheek. Alec turned his face into her hand and pressed his lips to her palm. Then he buried his fingers in her silky curls and tilted her face to his. Sliding her hand up the plane of his chest, she linked her fingers behind his neck, and tugged his head down to hers.

"Everything my heart desires is right here," Tessa murmured against his lips. "What more could I possibly wish for?"

A word about the author...

Sharon Saracino was born and raised in beautiful Northeastern Pennsylvania. Always the girl with her nose in a book, a lifelong love of writing took a back seat to real life while she got married, raised a family, and finally decided what she wanted to be when she grew up! She frequently announced that someday she was going to write a book. One milestone birthday (we won't discuss which one!) she decided someday would be here and gone if she didn't get her butt in gear. She plans to win the lottery just as soon as she remembers to purchase a ticket, fantasizes about moving to Italy, brews limoncello, and believes there's always magic to be found if you only take the time to look for it!

Thank you for purchasing
this publication of The Wild Rose Press, Inc.

If you enjoyed the story, we would appreciate your
letting others know by leaving a review.

For other wonderful stories,
please visit our on-line bookstore at
www.thewildrosepress.com.

For questions or more information
contact us at
info@thewildrosepress.com.

The Wild Rose Press, Inc.
www.thewildrosepress.com

Stay current with The Wild Rose Press, Inc.

Like us on Facebook

https://www.facebook.com/TheWildRosePress

And Follow us on Twitter
https://twitter.com/WildRosePress